LUVONE

AN ANTHOLOGY OF SHORT STORIES

Copyright © 2021
Email: luvonestories@gmail.com

ISBN: 978-0-620-92720-8

Printed in South Africa by Creda Communications

CONTENTS

FOREWORD

A writer is an incredibly lonely craftsperson who operates in solitude and silence away from the rest of the world. Writing is also an intimate affair: we choose to tell the stories that matter to us. But what happens to them at the end of the day? Who fans the fire of the writer, gives them a chance, direction and motivation? Those who have walked the path know the darkness - now let there be light. That is exactly what *Luvone* means in TjiKalanga: LAMP/LIGHT.

The Luvone Short Story competition was conceived from a desire to promote Zimbabwean writing; to help younger aspiring creators find their footing and encourage them to keep telling their stories. It was a dream that could not have come this far without the generosity of the wider community, mainly in Zimbabwe and its diaspora.

To ensure quality in the adjudication process, I needed to get competent people and have them focused enough to sift through the huge pile of submissions. Furthermore, prizes for the writers were needed and all this could not have been done without the generous support of our well-wishers; I thank them deeply.

I was truly overwhelmed by the response, both from the public and the writers who submitted their entries. The inaugural competition received over 100 submissions from the Bulawayo, Matabeleland South and Matabeleland North Provinces. There are plans to go national, but given the response, there was wisdom in starting small and local; to learn how to grow from there. The project is off to a great start; these efforts are only a drop in the ocean.

After the competition was done, I decided to put this collection together. From all the submissions, twenty-five entries were selected, later trimmed to a long list of fifteen and then down to the final four prize winners. *Body 215* by *Kimberly T. Moyo* received first place and the three runners up were *Into Paradise* by *Andile A. Dube, Divine Strings* by *Ashton R.M. Khumalo* and *Black Diamond* by *Lubelihle Sibanda*.

Stories in this anthology are from the top fifteen entries. All the writers are aged between eighteen and twenty-five and such amazing stories they tell! Such talent! Such light! I would like to extend my congratulations to them, you are now published!

On behalf of the team and the supporting community, I congratulate each featured writer for coming this far, and the bravery it took to bare your souls to the world at the risk of judgement, scrutiny, ridicule and vulnerability. All the best on your journey, keep on sharing your light, Luvone.

Last but not least, my sincerest gratitude goes to my co-editors, Busisekile Khumalo and Philani A. Nyoni, renowned and celebrated Zimbabwean authors. This wouldn't have been possible without you.

YVONNE MAPHOSA
Founder of the Luvone Short Stories Competition

BODY 215

Kimberly Thabisiwe Moyo

"**A**re you seeing things again Nhlaka?" taunted Shelly as she swigged her miniature bottle of whisky, before quickly stashing it back into her lab coat.

I muttered some nasty words to her, under my breath as I left the tea room for the morgue. Ever since my colleagues heard about my calling they had not given me a break. I had been the topic of every conversation at Hope-Fountain Mortuary and I felt like my head was going to explode. I was fatigued and emotionally drained. I mean have you tried explaining how you can communicate with your ancestors, to a group of American pathologist, who also happen to be devout scientific realists? Trust me it's not easy.

As I approached the Left Wing I noticed the morgue door was wide open, yet again!

"What part of 'close the door' do you College students not understand?" I yelled at the group of nervous medical students, who most likely did not have the authority to enter the morgue anyway, but I was having too much of a bad day to care. I locked the door behind me and strode to locker 215. As soon as I touched the handle I felt butterflies flutter in my stomach. I shrugged it off and pulled the locker door open.

The moment I laid my eyes on the body, I abruptly jerked forward, slamming my head against the metal operation table and tearing my forehead open. I fell to the cold marble floor, shaking violently like a headless chicken. I kicked the crash trolley over with my left foot, hurling the surgical instruments across the room. Warm foam rose in my throat, sending me into a coughing fit. Almost simultaneously my tongue ballooned to twice its size, blocking my airway. My own hands tightened around my neck as the distorted images of Body 215 being strangled filled my head. I frantically tried shaking myself out of the nightmare as my heart pounded erratically in my chest.

The vision hadn't changed. I kept seeing the same creased, muscular hands with an extremely distinct gold watch, wrapped around the young woman's neck. The hands seemed almost transparent. I couldn't tell whether they belonged to a white or black man. The way the woman writhed in pain as she gasped for breath was in sync with how I was squirming on the floor as I choked on my spit. It was like I had entered her body. I could feel her pain and fear. Sweat drenched my entire body. Her piercing screams filled my head until they turned into muffled moans. As peacefully as her soul left her body, my hands dropped from my neck and I stopped shaking. I lay motionless on the floor as my chest heaved up and down. This feeling was one I could never get used to.

"I must have strangled myself too much this time," I chuckled at my dark humour. The gaping slash in my forehead was throbbing immensely. I clumsily stood up to wash my face and felt warm blood trickle into my eye and all over my lab coat.

As I washed my face I kept trying to put the pieces of this confusing puzzle together. Americans did not have active ancestors like ours, so why was I having visions of this woman's death? Why were the perpetrator's hands transparent? There were just so many questions but the biggest mystery was the watch. It was unique and stood out like a diamond in the mud. Ever since the visions started, I had looked over every wrist I walked past. In the train, at work and the grocery store. I even got distracted one Sunday at church as I scanned the congregation's wrists while delivering the Offering Message. With the way my eyes darted from one hand to another, one would swear I was a pickpocket looking for my next unfortunate target.

I was so lost in my thoughts that I had not noticed the sink running over with bloody water.

"Great, another mess to clean up," I sighed as I hastily closed the tap and took the mop.

The body was still on the locker table where I had left it before my 'little incident'. I don't even know why I had come back here to torture myself. It was apparent from the purple bruises on her neck and her crushed oesophagus that she had died of asphyxiation. My job as a pathologist was done. All I had to do, was find out the cause of death and call it a day but I don't know why I was still here trying to find out whodunit.

"Because your job as a Sangoma has just begun, my child," the whisper of my grandmother's voice cascaded the room. I suddenly felt comforted. I had a purpose. My gift wasn't a mistake. No matter what anyone said, I was unique in a way none of them could ever fathom. I, Nhlakanipho Ntombiyolwandle Nxumalo, was chosen by my ancestors to carry out their work on earth and I was going to prove that when I found out who killed this poor young lady and why.

I glanced back at the body. It was a mess. A monstrous blow to her lower face had dislocated her jawbone. Her left eye was the deepest shade of black I had ever seen. She had a barcode tattooed under her collarbone and the words 'King Ricky' on her inner bottom lip. Every inch of her body had piercings, from her eyelids to her nipples. She was covered in a mass of scars and bruises probably from whippings. A jagged piece of bone stuck out of her broken rib cage. Her injuries, the branding tattoos, along with the red corset she was wearing when she was brought in, made me conclude that she was a prostitute. They always ended up dead like this, violently, and usually in the hands of someone they knew. It was either a gang, drug or pimp related murder.

I heard a key turn in the door before a surprised

Shelly stumbled in.

"Oh, you are in here?" she snorted while freely gulping the last of her whisky.

"You need to get help."

"That will be my New Year's Resolution," she winked sarcastically.

Shelly had a growing addiction to alcohol. I only found out after stumbling across her stash which she hid behind the lockers in the morgue. She concealed her secret so well that no one knew. Not even her parents or her boyfriend Uche. I did not like Uche. He was one of those imprecise guys. You could never really tell what he was up to. He was, in his own words 'an entrepreneur slash hustler'. The latter probably referred to drug dealing, theft and some other dodgy business. What I couldn't understand though was how Shelly Munroe, a whole qualified pathologist with a successful career, a big house and two cars in her name could fall for a troublemaker like him.

"So were you chatting with your Gods again?" she asked as she refilled her whisky bottle which she disguised as Apple Energade.

"Ancestors Shelly, they are ancestors, not Gods."

"Yeah them, have they told you what happened to the girl?"

"No, not yet, but the visions are getting stronger. I just need to find that distinct-"

"It's Uche's birthday on Monday. What do you think I should get him?" she blurted out as she fixed her hair in the mirror.

"I don't know, he's your boyfriend," I replied, annoyed that she had not been listening to me.

"But you're African, you know what Africans like."

"Shelly, Africa isn't some tiny village. Uche is from Nigeria, I'm from Zimbabwe. That's like Texas and New York. That's two different countries. So I couldn't possibly know what Nigerians like to get on their birthday!" I snapped, before slamming the door and leaving a stunned Shelly behind me.

Shelly was my only friend here but she was also the most annoying person I had ever met.

I spent most of the weekend burning incense and summoning my ancestors to ask them for guidance. This was my first vision since my initiation ceremony back home. It was tremendously significant as it would determine my future as a reputable Sangoma. I was nervous that I would mess it up. What worried me the most was the absence of my instructor. I felt so alone. I hadn't eaten much for days. I had eye bags big enough to fit oranges and I looked at least twenty years older.

I had also run out of excuses for keeping the body at the morgue. Since it was a homicide case it had to be handed over to the police but thank God for Shelly. She was the only person who didn't think I was weird or possessed. She couldn't quite understand what I was going through but she had done a good job holding back the Body Transfer Process for me, but I only had up to Monday. The pressure was on.

My shoulders were tense and in desperate need of a massage. Every inch of my body was in knots. After a long mint soak in the bathtub, I retired for bed. Falling asleep was pretty challenging for me lately. Insomnia had taken over my life. After much tossing and turning, I eventually managed to shut an eye. Just as my alarm went off, I had a vivid dream of the day Shelly introduced me to Uche, which was a few months ago. I shrugged it off as I got ready for work.

Monday mornings at Hope-Fountain Mortuary were very peaceful. There was none of that Monday Buzz that everyone in the corporate world always grumbled about. In fact, it was my favourite day of the workweek. Since it wasn't busy I decided to grab a chair and go sit outside for some much needed clean air.

I chose a spot under a leafy maple tree. It had rained the night before and the fresh scent of wet sand filled the garden. There was a termite mound by the tree trunk. It reminded me of the sand back home which I was craving a lot lately. There wasn't any nice sand in America. I chuckled at the thought of my neighbours seeing me digging for sand, to eat. They would most certainly bring me dozens of food baskets thinking I was dying of starvation.

My head was filled with happy thoughts for a moment until I started wondering what exactly I was going to do when I found out what happened to that girl. It's not like I could go to the police and tell them my ancestors had shown me a vision. That wouldn't even stand in court. If anything I would make it to 'This week's funniest videos' on the Daily Show. I couldn't approach the culprit either.

Having a gift like my mine was tough especially in a foreign country like America. I didn't even bother explaining what it was like anymore. I just let people run with whatever they assumed, because every time I tried to, I would get lectured about science and how dead people don't communicate with the living. One lady even went to the extent of freely offering me her services as a psychiatrist! Some people though, like my old widowed neighbour Mrs Reeds was so interested that she would bring me beads every time she went to the market. I didn't even use beads in my practice but it was the thought that counted.

As I continued pondering my thoughts I spotted Shelly's shiny black Chevrolet pulling into the parking lot. She was late, as usual, but wasn't even in a rush. She hooted at me to come over to her car. I certainly did not feel like standing up. The soft wind was so cooling. I was now dozing off and actually felt sleepy for the first time in days. Shelly continued hooting like a wedding motorcade with a bride. I hurriedly got to my feet to shut her up because she was now making a scene. Besides annoying, my dear friend was also a drama queen. I smiled to myself as I strolled to her car.

"You do know this is Dr García's parking spot, right?" I asked her as I climbed into the passenger's seat.

"I know that's why I parked here."

"Why do you like causing trouble, Shelly?" I snickered.

"Because it's fun! I can't wait for him to come shouting down the corridor asking who parked in his spot."

We both laughed hysterically at the thought of this. Dr García was such a cranky old man, he had earned a few humorous nicknames. The student doctors called him El Chapo because he was Mexican. On his moody days, they would joke about how his drugs were probably stuck at the border.

"I finally got something for Uche's birthday."

"Hmm, what did you get?" I rolled my eyes.

It was not a secret that I did not like him. He just was not good enough for her. He had no house, car or a steady job. What he did have however was a lot of rowdy friends who were just as aimless as he was. Even the phone he used was bought by Shelly. He had told her that he was in the process of starting a car dealership company. With the rate at which cars were going missing in the neighbourhood, I was one hundred per cent sure he was stealing them. I, however, made sure not to say this because Shelly believed everything that came out of his mouth.

She rummaged through her handbag and took out a small black box that looked like it had a ring in it. I raised my eyebrow at her.

"No man, I'm not going to ask him to marry me," she laughed

I opened it and froze. My mind raced like a motorbike as I tried to comprehend what was going on. My stomach stiffened and churned into a tight knot. The top of my ears heated up so fast you could fry an egg on them. Panic engulfed me. I was breathing so rapidly it felt like an asthma attack. I could feel myself losing control of my body. I didn't know whether I wanted to scream or cry. My hands started quivering like a leaf in the wind.

"Nhlaka are you okay?" Shelly asked worriedly.

"Where did you get this?" My voice was now raspy and I could barely hear myself speak.

"I got it custom made from the-. Why are you shaking like that?"

"Shelly this, this is the watch." I stuttered.

"What watch?"

I jolted out of my seat, convulsing viciously before I could respond to her. I couldn't even feel her hands as she tried to get me out of the car and onto the ground. All I could see was Uche wringing the life out of the body in Locker 215.

KIMBERLY THABISIWE MOYO was born in 1998 and has lived in Harare, Victoria Falls and now Bulawayo, Zimbabwe. Growing up she enjoyed scrap-booking and swimming. She has won several Public Speaking competitions, including 1st Runner up in the 2017 Skyz Metro Competition. If she isn't drawing, she is binge watching unsolved murder mysteries. **Body 215** is her first published short story.

INTO PARADISE

Andile Austin Dube

Sizwe traversed the avenues of a hollow dream with the hopes of getting to the little voices giggling in the dark miasma. He looked in every direction and there he saw them in the distance, his two little daughters holding hands. He tried calling out to them but the turbulent hiss of water crashing on rocks drowned his yells until he could no longer hear himself. He sat up at once in great confusion as he woke from his deplorable nightmare. The water hissing in his dream was real, it was the Limpopo on whose wet bank he unknowingly lay, phasing in and out of a fiendish stupor. He was quick to notice that his toes were in the wind, they had spared not even his shoes.

"Sthandwa!" he shouted into the dawn.

His missing shoes were a great problem but not as great as his missing wife. Earlier on, he had been sent into a gentle slumber by the soft jazz playing through the speakers of Toyota Quantum which was supposed to clandestinely smuggle them into South Africa. He circled around in great panic until the bush leaves around him started rustling, sending a shudder down his spine. He struck one of the very few match sticks in his pocket and pointed the flickering flame in the direction from whence the noise came.

"Who is there?" he asked with a quavering voice.

"It's me Baba, don't hurt me," replied a tall man as he emerged from the bushes.

His frame was almost skeletal, the muddy water was the only thing keeping him alive. Sizwe rushed to help the guy as he staggered towards him. He sat him gently on the ground and soon had a fire going.

"Why are you alone? What are you doing here?" Sizwe asked the stranger.

"My sister," he replied, "They took her."

"They also took my wife," great concern and sorrow laced Sizwe's voice, "I regret leaving home but I couldn't bear the poverty after the elections."
The stranger sat himself upright despite the agony.
"I too couldn't stand the suffering after they closed the borders because of Covid."
"What is Covid?" Sizwe was clearly perturbed by what the other man mentioned.
"A deadly malady my friend," replied the stranger, "how come you know not of it?"
Sizwe was lost in the conversation. He thought that maybe the hunger and disorientation had made the stranger a bit mad.
The stranger groaned in pain as he asked, "What elections do you speak of my friend?"
"The 2008 elections, which ones could I possibly speak of?" replied Sizwe.
The stranger too was lost in the conversation, even scared of the barefooted man in his presence.
"The only deadly malady back home is cholera," Sizwe said as he beat out the fire in the morning sun.
"2008 was twelve years ago my friend," the stranger sounded hesitant as if he were afraid of angering Sizwe.
Sizwe was quiet for a while, processing the stranger's words. He had left for South Africa in August of 2008 and here before him was a man speaking of unknown maladies and future times.
"I am planning to cross the river today, are you coming with?" Sizwe asked the ailing stranger, "maybe we might catch wind of our kin."
"I am too weak to cross my friend," responded the stranger with very little conviction, as if signifying how weak he is.
"I will carry you," Sizwe insisted until the stranger hesitantly nodded.
He hauled him over his broad shoulders and headed straight towards the mighty river. The water

brushed against his beard as he dragged his feet in the deep. He would gulp a cupful of Limpopo from time to time. The water was neither bitter nor sweet, it was just plain maybe in an effort to conceal its morbid tales. The force rushing beside him became so great that he started gulping bucket loads.

"Put me down my friend," begged the stranger, "go on and find your wife."

Sizwe never replied, he just shook his head in disapproval of the stranger's sacrificial thoughts. His nose was now below the water but he kept on until he tripped on a boulder below the surface of the water. The stranger slowly floated away but Sizwe grabbed him by the tip of his fingers.

"Let go my friend, it was nice knowing you!" shouted the stranger.

Sizwe held on tightly until he started hearing the little voices giggling in the distance.

"My girls," he muttered as he looked over to the stranger. "I'm sorry," he said as he let go of the stranger.

He dragged himself on the riverbed for what seemed to be forever. He looked over to the stranger still floating away in the distance and he could not help but notice airy fountains of water shooting beside the stranger. It was the hippos! Sizwe looked away in deep regret and continued towards the bank on the other side. He could not feel his legs as he lay on the wet sand. He opened his water-logged eyes and there in the shrubs beside him was what looked like his shoes. They were very old, the leather had even lost its elasticity and shine. When he held them, they crumbled into a rubbery powder due to their weathered state.

The words of the stranger kept on ringing in his mind.

"2008 was twelve years ago," the stranger had said.

He left them as they were, his bare feet would do a better job after all. Before he could figure out his next move, the ground beneath him started vibrating and on the plain ahead of him was a border patrol helicopter. Ten men who were armed to the teeth descended from it and started fanning out to cover different positions. He felt his legs once again out of necessity and he ran for his dear life. Shots were ringing in the distance and he ran till he could not hear the echoes of the muzzles. Chaos unravelled in the trees as the patrols and the smugglers fought it off. Sizwe sat beside a huge dry tree when a gang of smugglers ran beside him. He curled up into a ball beside the path but it was too late to hide. They ran beside him but none of them seemed to notice him. He stood up and noticed that even the border patrol men did not care about him. He took the opportunity to distance himself from this malevolent chaos.

He sat beside a huge rock and squeezed his t-shirt into his mouth to drink the little water and sweat he had accumulated. Heavy clouds gathered from the south and Sizwe looked around and saw that he was in the open. He removed his torn t-shirt and suspended it on the branches to protect himself from the coming rain. The wind blew the t-shirt off and he was out in the open again. At this point he had lost all hope so he staggered further south in the icy rain without shoes and a t-shirt. Through the rain, he saw two little girls giggling and he followed their chatter.

"My girls," he said with a shivering smile on his face.

The giggling slowly turned into cries. He crawled over a rock following the sounds of crying women. He was met by a pretty disturbing view. Scores of barely dressed women were lined up out in the open with the rain pounding heavily on them. There were three men marching around them with *sjamboks* in their hands.

"Take a bath you filthy Zimbabweans!" shouted one of the men.

A fourth man appeared from a makeshift tent and chose one of the women to keep him company in the cold rainy weather. She refused and sjambok strokes descended on her until she could not stand anymore. The men dragged her into the tent and there she yelled in pain as they had their way with her. Sizwe broke down into tears. He knew he was outnumbered to do anything.

He whispered, "Sthandwa!" with the hopes that one of the women was his wife.

When all the men were inside the tent feasting on the unlucky woman, Sizwe descended from the huge rock into the women. He ordered them to free their bindings and run but none of them seemed to respond or even acknowledge his presence.

"They can't see you," said a voice from behind.

He turned around to discover that the voice was from the stranger he had let go of earlier on. The stranger was draped in clean laboratory coat with antiseptic gloves.

"But you---,"

"Drowned, yes," replied the stranger, "That was part of the whole experiment!"

The stranger walked up to touch one of the women's faces and his hand just went through the face as if the woman was just a projection.

"You are in the Institute of Higher Brain Research in South Africa. You have never heard of us because we are a government secret. Our work is what you might call unethical but believe me, it's for the greater good."

"I don't understand," Sizwe mumbled as he looked around the smuggler's compound.

"Twelve years ago, we found you dying by the Limpopo riverbed. You begged us to save you, even signed up to be our guinea pig given that we save your wife," the stranger explained.

As he spoke, Sizwe's surroundings started disintegrating and he saw a reflection of himself in the Toyota Quantum once again.

Soft jazz music was playing through the speakers and there Sizwe sat with his wife and a few other men and women. The music was making him doze off from time to time.

"So why are you doing this?" asked one of the passengers referring to the illegal crossing they were undertaking.

"I have two daughters. One is ten and the other twelve. I have to give them a better future," Sizwe replied.

"I'm a teacher and I can no longer fend for my family too, I hope to find a stable teaching job or even a toilet cleaning one," the passenger revealed as he stretched his hand, "I'm Samuel Ndlovu, beside me is my sister, Mary."

"Dr Sizwe Ncube, my wife Sthandwa," replied Sizwe as he too reached out for Samuel's hand.

"Doctor, you are too educated to be among us," Samuel said jokingly.

"Where I'm from it no longer matters Samuel," Sizwe replied sadness coating his words.

The smooth ride suddenly became bumpy indicating a shift of terrain. The music went off and the driver switched off the headlights to avoid attracting unnecessary attention to the car. In the middle of nowhere, the car stopped and very unfriendly men banged on it instructing everyone to get out. The mood suddenly changed, the smugglers were no longer nice.

"Okay, gentlemen, we will cross with the ladies first then you will follow behind," said one of the smugglers whom they kept on referring to as Dlozi.

"What difference does it make?" Samuel asked in protest.

Dlozi did not take lightly to being disrespected in front of his subordinates. He turned around to collect his composure. Dlozi's men descended on Samuel with fists and kicks. Sizwe was shocked by the sudden hostility but he could not risk being beaten in front of his wife. Mary wept uncontrollably until the men stuffed her mouth with a bathing towel. Samuel groaned in agony as the men continuously assaulted him. Dlozi raised his hand and they stopped.

"I was trying to reduce the pain on your part my friends but one of you disrespected me. This is the last time you will ever see your wives or sisters or whatever," Dlozi said in a loathsome tone.

As he spoke, his goons grabbed all the men and forced them to drink a bitter liquid which stirred up a pretty wrangle in their stomachs.

"We have been played. They are not smugglers. They are traffickers!" shouted Sizwe as he passed out.
It was dark for an eternity and Sizwe woke up beside the river from a very unpleasant dream. He had not the slightest idea of how he had ended up there. He struck a couple of his wet match sticks in fear when the trees around him started rustling.

"Sthandwa!" he shouted.
A very beat up man showed up from behind the shrubs. It was Sizwe's fellow passenger from earlier on.

"Samuel! How long have we been asleep?" asked Sizwe.

"I don't know my friend. They took her, they took my sister," said Samuel as he cried.

"I'm planning to cross the river, maybe we might catch wind of our kin. Do you want to come with?" asked Sizwe.

"I'm too weak," Samuel replied.

"I will carry you," Sizwe insisted.

"Stop!" Sizwe shouted at the stranger with the lab coat, "I let him drown, didn't I?"

The projections stopped moving and they disintegrated into nothing. The two were standing in a very huge and bright white hall. All sorts of probes and wires were sticking out of Sizwe's head and high above in an observation window were more scientists taking notes.

"We are looking for better ways to suppress traumatic memories for accident survivors, war veterans and for children who would have witnessed a tragic event. When I first heard your story, I knew you were the perfect subject for my experiments," the stranger said with a stolid face, "every year we erase your memories and subject you to that one event when you left Samuel to drown. We try to give you clues that your world is not real, for example, telling you that 2008 was twelve years ago but your brain still insists that you cross the river and relive the drowning again and again."

"What about the helicopter and women in the traffickers' compounds?" Sizwe asked.

"The helicopter is how we rescued you. We had a brief shoot out with the traffickers. We found you curled up on the ground next to the river. You told us what had happened and that led us to your wife on that rainy day in the compound. You offered to work with us instead of being arrested and the results we yielded from earlier versions of this experiment helped us to suppress your wife's memories of abuse and rape during her transit into paradise and now she is the happiest woman you can never know."

"What happened to my daughters?" Sizwe asked.

"Come with me," motioned the stranger. Scientists helped Sizwe out of the electrodes sticking out of his brain and the two men walked out of the white hall into a huge SUV car. They finally pulled up near a huge fancy house in Sandton. There was a small family party in the backyard and everyone there was happy.

"That is your older daughter and her husband. She is twenty-four now and happily married to an accountant. The little girl with them is your granddaughter," said the stranger as he pointed out to them. Another girl came out of the house carrying a huge cake.

"That is your other daughter, she is twenty-two now and studying to be a medical doctor."

Sizwe was in tears at this point, tears of joy. Lastly, a lady came out of a car with a man about her age. Sizwe's face brightened as he saw her.

"That's your wife Sthandwa and her husband. She remarried five years after you last saw her," said the stranger, "they all believe that you passed away, showing up will ruin their happiness forever my friend."

Sizwe looked at his family one last time and went into the car a happy man. The car disappeared over the horizon leaving behind the happy family.

ANDILE AUSTIN DUBE is an Engineering student at the National University of Science and Technology (NUST). Although inclined to the subject, he spends most of his time writing short stories, in particular the Horror and Sci-Fi genre. He started writing at the age of 10 for the satisfaction which came with creating one's own characters, world and rules. His favourite authors are Shirley Jackson and Ernest Hemingway whose style of writing is quite distinct and very vivid.

BLACK DIAMOND
Lubelihle Sibanda

Stealthily, I tiptoe towards my prey. Careful not to make a sound, I slither my foot against the grass with the adopted skill of a calculative snake. My prey is so close, I can even feel its breath brushing against the hairs on my face. I am invisible. My whole body is coated with green slime obtained from crushed herbs, that way I have easily merged with the forest. Like a chameleon, I play hide and seek. Too bad for this impala, it's a game of blood, I hide and kill. As I gather all my energy in preparation for a single attack, my muscles bulge out and my eyes turn red like those of a charging bull. The beast in me is awakened. It only takes a fraction of a second for me to spring on top of my prey. I strike faster than the sting of a scorpion.

While my body is in the air, wrestling against the pull of gravity, I unfold my hands and aim for the neck. I release all the strength from my muscles and tighten my grip. My jaw tightens. I clench my teeth and bite my lower lip. I can feel the life of the helpless animal fading away. I am invincible. No man can dare challenge me in this village. Strength is something I was naturally born with.

As I slice my impala into portions, questions exchange greetings in my buzzing head. How does it feel like to be dead? Just a little splash of blood and a little pain here and there. How painful can death be? What happens when I die? Will I see my spirit float away from my lifeless body? Will I be carried into an emotionless world? A world of unmitigated numbness? Don't get me wrong, I am not having suicidal thoughts. I don't want to die. Not when I'm still a virgin. Never! I am only nineteen, I have not yet enjoyed the pleasures of this world. Grandma Mthimbeni, I prefer calling her Gogo, once told me that the dead are around us, watching over us, protecting us from evil spirits that hover over the soils of Imkhuba translated as, 'the village of Habits.' She even told me that the dead become our ancestors after they embark on a spiritual journey. I remember, she also mentioned that the people who did good deeds on earth are led to the white path and eventually get transformed into good spirits which are our ancestors. Looking far ahead and staring into nothing, I release a small laugh of disbelief. What does Gogo know? It's not like she has ever died before, how could she possibly know all of that? The old woman must be losing it. I don't blame her, surely, her ninety-seven year old brain has retired by now.

Everything about this village is mysterious. Straight up from the people, down to the land, chickens and lizards. Everything is strange if not abnormal. You cannot look at any creeping thing that lives in Imkhuba and not put a big question mark on it. Look at Gogo for instance. Most of the time you would find her kneeling right in the middle of the path that leads to the river, her skeleton of a body roasting in the blazing sun. I swear our village was wrongly named, this must be the real Kalahari. You would find Gogo dripping wet with perspiration. The first time I saw her like that, I thought maybe someone had baptised her with a calabash of water but no, she had incinerated herself in the sun all in the name of "speaking to the invisible." I clap my hands in amazement. Crazy is the normal in this village.

Imagine if you were a visitor to my village, and you came across an old woman kneeling in the middle of the path. When I say old, I mean ninety-seven years plus only God knows how many more. The age we all know is just the minimum estimation. Imagine looking at how her parched lips move in vigorous motion as she utters nothing. Just picture her shiny and almost transparent scalp, believe me, her skull is almost visible. Visualise her head, jerking upwards and in every other direction as if she's seeing flying ghosts. The off-white hairs on her scalp, I can count with my fingers. No wonder we have never had a single soul coming to visit our land. If we ever get one, our donkeys would stop urinating in our drinking well.

"You have the audacity, the nerve to hunt in my territory!"

A man from nowhere barks at me, his spit showering my back. From his tone I can detect arrogance and pompousness. He better not try me. I am in too good of a mood to knock someone's teeth out today. He better not look for my trouble.

"Are you deaf? I am talking to you, you idiot! This is my territory. That impala is mine!"

"Is your name written in any of the bushes around here?" I sneer at him while I shoot him a *do not try me* look over my shoulder. He remains silent.

"Thought so too," I say.

"Who do you think you are, you think I am afraid of you?" He is looking down at me, while his chest is puffed up like that of an angry frog. His chest muscles are vibrating and his lips are quivering with irritation.

"That, my brother, is not a choice. You must fear me," I respond.

I have already balled my fists, prepared to teach this rat some manners.

My instincts are sharp, I sense his attack. I turn around quickly and catch his flying fist right in the middle of its track. My lips twitch and freeze into one nasty grin. He gasps in shock. I then unleash a mighty blow that connects straight to his jaw. I hear a cracking sound of things breaking and falling out of place. Two of his teeth spring out of his mouth, along with a shower of blood. My blow sends him reeling to the grass.

Nxx! I click my tongue in disgust.

I leave him screaming like a little girl on the ground. I look at him in distaste.

"Then you call yourself a man."

I hang my meat on a stick and carry it on my shoulder and head home.

Two days ago, Gogo took my hands and looked at my palms. It was as if she was reading something in them. She smiled at me more radiantly than I had ever seen before. She beamed at me. The tender skin on her cheeks lifted, her mouth revealed toothless gums. Her eyes shone like those of a happy infant. Then she told me I was special. I look at my hands now and wonder what she saw. I only see pierces and scratches I got from fetching Mopani worms and strangling animals to death with my bare hands. I so vividly remember, the way she took her walking stick and walked like a tortoise, heading for the forest. Her saggy and droopy breasts wobbled as she carefully placed one foot after the other. Her breasts looked like shrivelled bananas. As I am thinking of that, I cup my own breasts with my hands. They are firm and perfectly round. I mutter a ridiculous silent prayer, please don't droop to that extent, please.

Oh, where are my manners? Let me introduce myself. If you were to paint a picture of me, you might want to use a darker shade of pencil, with a sharp pang of attitude. My skin is like that of the dark mud found in the nooks and crannies of Imkhuba River. An African child, they say, but I prefer being called the 'black diamond.' I am a rare breed. I am a woman with guts. A woman worthy to be a man. A girl who sheds blood every month but never a tear. Besides being stubborn, egocentric and mean, I have other good traits too. I am a goddess of beauty, my body butternut curved, lips plump, raised cheekbones and eyes that scream fire. My birth name is Dumie, short for Dumisa. It means 'Praise'.

Hidden behind this coat of aggressiveness and ego is a lonely heart searching for a touch of love. My age mates are all married, happily I guess. Well I don't really care, I lie to myself. What would I need a man for? I have the strength to protect myself.

That little voice in my head betrays me again. It whispers the bitter truth I don't want to hear.

You want love, Dumie.

Growing up was hard for me. From an early age of five, I was already showing traits of a warrior. My friends used to play with dolls made out of clay, which I found most boring and lame. I was always up for a challenge. I wanted to wrestle, to fight and just go wild. One by one, my friends left me. No girl wanted to fight, especially when we reached adolescence. They used to say no man wants to marry a fighter. I always felt out of place. It felt wrong to be me.

Like I said before, I am a goddess of beauty. When I walk in the village centre, heads turn around. Men look at me lustfully, like dogs looking at a piece of meat hanging on the tree. Yet, because of a terrible rumour that has polluted the whole village, men no longer dare look my way twice. People believe the reason behind my strength is that I have a spirit of a man living inside me.

"Nxx! They can go to hell for all I care."

"So this is how you will always be? Huh? Will you spend the rest of your life clicking your tongue? Nxx!"
Did she just click her tongue too? Well I can say it's in the DNA of African people.

That's my mother over there. She shoots me a sharp look and I quickly put my legs together. I don't need another preaching on how a girl is supposed to sit. Mama's rebukes always come in a series of emphasis.

"Dumie! Will you sit like that when we get visitors in this hut? With your legs wide open like that, ngweeee for everyone to see? Your father must be turning in his grave. I keep telling you to close..." on and on the sermon goes. Whenever this happens, I put her on mute, just stare at her as if I would be listening to anything she says.

"Did you hear a word I said?" She'd shout and I would just nod my head.

Well, seems like today I saved myself from the chastening by quickly sitting properly. I watch her toss the impala meat in sesame oil, preparing to grill it over the hot charcoal in the fireplace. Unlike me, she cooks very well. Her food is always tasty. Lately, she has stopped complaining about me and my hunting habits.

"Dumie, you better return that dead thing you are carrying on your shoulder to where it came from. What kind of a girl are you? Cook, you feed us poison. Sweep, you scratch my compound with a broom. Simply girl tasks, you cannot do yet you run after men's duties. Tell me, who will want to marry you?"

She used to shout at me every time I hunted. My mother's beauty disappears when she gets angry. Her eyes almost pop out of her sockets, not forgetting the showers of spit that baptise me every time she barks into my face.

Well, hunger always humbles a person. These days, she has been the one reminding me that I haven't gone hunting yet. She has turned a deaf ear to her friends who tell her that she should not allow me to do manly things. She can be stubborn sometimes. She is hard headed this one. Indeed, an apple does not fall far from the tree.

After devouring my meal. I stand up and walk out of the hut for some air. I watch as the sun kisses the end of the sky. The night is beautiful. What makes the darkness look bad are the evil things people do in the dark.

I can hear crickets making their own music and owls getting ready to be sent to their allocated shrines by the witches. Witchcraft exists. I have seen a witch with my own eyes. If Gogo does not fit your own description of a witch then I don't know what else does. Like I said, this is a strange village. At night, screams of people at war and baby cries are heard all over the place, when you go out of the hut to look you hear nothing. By the time you lay your head down again to get some sleep, it starts again. I have gotten used to it, in fact, it has now become my lullaby.

As I place my head on my folded arm, I am instantly drawn away into the dreamland.

I let myself dive deep into an empty void.

My whole body is electrified by a shock of pleasure. I can feel his hands torturing my skin with feelings I cannot explain as he traces his fingertips up to my breasts. Slowly, he gently cups them. My nipples stand firm and rigid in response to the touch of his cold hands. His teeth go for my neck. The pain of his teeth sinking into my flesh is painful but surprisingly it feels so good. I let down my guard and just surrender to his demands. I cannot see his face. He is standing behind me, his muscular body pressed against my back. I can feel his erection poking my buttocks. He lets go of my breasts and starts lifting up my skirt with his fingertips. I start feeling hot. I cannot even tell him to stop, I don't want him to. I start sweating, the heat is getting too much. Beads of sweat form on my forehead. What is he doing to me? The heat increases. No, this is becoming a nightmare.

This man, this stranger, suddenly becomes aggressive. His hands go for my throat. He starts choking me. I wriggle vigorously, fighting for air. I grab his hands, trying to get them off my neck. It's no use. Flashes of memory, glimpses of vague ephemeral images swoosh through my mind. I see my own hands on an animal's throat. I feel like the victim now. Tables have turned. My questions are now being answered. So this is how death feels like. From another dimension, I can see my eyes dimming. It's like I am in another realm. I can see my body, my spirit is outside my body. Then I feel like I am sinking, deep into a trench of vipers. Owls seem to be laughing at my doom. I now see different animals coming towards me with eyes full of mercilessness. I have never felt this scared and vulnerable in my life. For the first time teardrops flood my eyes and spill over, chasing each other down my pale cheeks.

His grip on my neck keeps getting tighter. I am losing the strength to fight back. From nowhere, I start to feel someone else's hands trying to remove mine from my neck. Wait. Are there two of these strangers trying to kill me?

A hot slap lands on my face and I spring up to my feet. My throat is sore and painful.

"I've been trying to wake you up," shouts my mother. "You were strangling yourself in sleep. We are under attack! We have to run!"

So that's why I was feeling so hot. Some people are trying to burn us alive in our hut. The roof is on fire. There is debris everywhere. We run for the door. Just as we manage to escape from the fire. A man grabs my mother, like an eagle snatching its prey off the ground. Terror seizes me by the throat. I release an amplified scream that echoes into the night.

I realise we are surrounded by a lot of men. I cannot identify their faces in this darkness as they stand in the shadows. My mother starts screaming in pain. That man is hurting her. He draws closer to me, so that I can see his face. He does this while dragging my mother by the neck. Tears form in my eyes. My heart skips a beat when I recognise that face. It's that man who fought me over his so-called territory and impala earlier today. The one who lost two of his teeth because of me.

"It's you," I say in utter shock. "Leave my mother alone you coward!" I scream. "It's me you're after!"

"Little girl, I am here to teach you a lesson before you greet your ancestors," he says while grinding his teeth.

My poor mother has already wet herself. She looks at me with teary eyes. She looks so fragile and helpless. I can hear her talking to me even if she's saying nothing.

"See what you have put us in. I told you to stay out of trouble. See what you have cost us?"

I can translate the message from the way she's looking at me. Now, I remember Gogo's words, you are special. What is special about me? I am cursed. How did I end up in this situation? Look at the pain I am putting my mother through.

The man lifts up a sharp knife and looks at it as if it's some piece of treasure.

"Any last words?" He sneers.

Gogo's words now echo louder in my eardrums, they now sound like a scream. You are special! You are special! You are special! I close my ears, the words are deafening. I'm sweating and panting heavily.

The man places the sharp knife against my mother's throat. Mama gasps in fear. I've never seen her this traumatised. My heart pounds a thousand prayers to every deity that was said to exist. Each accelerated heartbeat sends a plea of mercy to every ancestor of Imkhuba village.

LUBELIHLE SIBANDA is a passion driven young lady who aspires to be one of the greatest authors to ever walk the planet. She is a daring go-getter who has an attitude towards limits. She is an upcoming forensic psychologist, an actress, poet and chef.

DIVINE STRINGS

Ashton R.M Khumalo

The house was dark and silent when Ray went in. He just assumed his mother was already asleep but still he said, "Mom, I'm home! Hope you got my text!"

As he was about to turn on the lights in the sitting room, a silhouette caught his attention. His eyes began to acclimatise to the darkness, that's when his world stopped moving. He saw a man holding his mother in the air with one arm. With the little light that came in from outside, he could clearly make out her features. Her silk black hair all messed up, her sea blue eyes almost lifeless; she was partially drooling, and there was blood oozing from her neck where the man's thumb was. He saw her bare shoulder that should have been covered by her now torn dress that hung from one shoulder only; she had scratch marks on that bare shoulder, marks on which blood was clotted. Her arms were dangling by her sides, she didn't have any energy to even try and fight.

Ray saw her torn dress had been given an unprofessional vent, from the bottom below the knees, to just below her pelvic region. He saw the blood cascading from between his mother's legs. His eyes followed the red streams all the way down to her sole, and beyond that, to the floor. There was a small pool of blood below her that was steadily increasing in diameter. As his eyes took in the entire picture, Ray saw a strand of cloth that used to be his mom's underwear lying next to the sofa. He saw the shattered picture frames scattered all over the floor, he saw the fallen furniture. He saw eyes. Blood-red eyes looking back at him, eyes that seemed unreal, eyes that twinkled when they saw him see them.

"How nice of you to join us", the man spoke softly and kindly, grinning at Ray, paralysing him with his red eyes.

Ray's body froze. It was as if hearing those words turned the nightmare into reality; a bloody, messy, real reality. He just stood there by the sitting room entrance, watching, listening.

"I must admit, I did not anticipate an audience, dear boy, but you are very much welcome. This show is, after all, for anyone and everyone who can watch", the man said looking away from Ray.

Still Ray could not move.

"Now, if you'd be so kind as to stay there and not make a sound, I'd be truly grateful. Please, enjoy the show, my good sir."

With that, he looked at Ray again and briefly bowed his head before returning his full attention to Ray's mom. The man knew the boy would not do anything, he knew what fear could do to a person, especially fear entwined with confusion. He looked at his victim, she was a true beauty; he had memorised every feature of her gorgeous face before playing with her, so regardless of the few discrepancies on her face now, he would not let that dishearten him. In his heart of hearts, he knew she was a true beauty; and that was enough to get him thirsty for her again. He felt his boner growing and he licked his lips slowly.

Behave yourself, man! You have an audience now! he thought; looking at his groin and feeling embarrassed to find his zipper down.

"How clumsy of me, please do forgive me", he said to his petrified audience, pulling the zipper up.

Still Ray could not move.

The man suddenly lowered his victim and pulled her towards Ray, her feet being dragged across the floor, leaving a trail of blood. He stopped, "Perfect!" He then kicked down the small table, overturning it. The sudden thud startled Ray and he felt control over his body return to him. Before he could move, the man appeared suddenly before his face. The boy saw those eyes and just as quickly as he had owned his body, he lost that ownership and was paralysed yet again. The man returned to his position still holding Ray's mom in the air; it all happened so fast, Ray could have sworn he imagined those eyes before him.

"Now please let's not get excited and try anything, this is delicate work I'm doing. I need to stay focused, okay? So please don't move, like we had initially agreed", the man spoke softly again but this time with a hint of annoyance.

"As a responsible member of The Society, it is my duty to follow the rules and keep the peace going. For that to be, the only reasonable explanation for this entire ordeal, would be an animal attack; hence the show, my dear boy", he calmly said.

He ogled Ray's mother again, and slowly took his free hand inside the dress, between her legs. He fingered her for a short while before pulling his fingers out and licking them clean; all that while, Ray just watched and his mother remained lethargic. It was after licking the fingers that Ray noticed, for the first time, the claws on those fingers. With that free hand, the man proceeded to claw at the sofa making it seem like some wild animal had run over it and jumped. He then gently overturned the sofa, "Perfect! Just perfect. You should feel honoured, dear boy, it's not every day that someone gets to witness first-hand the creation of one of my masterpieces".

He looked around the room and when he was satisfied with the wild chaos it told, he beamingly said, "Behold! The final stroke on my canvas".

He clawed and scratched Mrs Tyler's face, almost ripping out her right eye. Still smiling, he began clawing randomly all over her upper body; then made a few scratches on her thighs. Finally, he focused all his artistry on her stomach. He vigorously clawed until her intestines started falling out. He then dropped her on the floor and made two more scratches on her neck. He stood up, took a step back and looked at his handy work.

"Beautiful!" He turned to Ray, "Now then," and started moving slowly towards him. Raymond looked at his mother, the last of his family. He felt more pain than what he had felt when he lost his father and brother. He had seen everything this animal had done to his mother, and he had felt rage, rage that he just stood there watching and did nothing. Only one feeling stood above his rage: Fear. Fear for his life; fear that he too, would face the same horrific fate. Fear that soon, the monster would be done with his mother and then he would be next. He had tried to force his body to run, his mouth to scream, his anything to do anything except watch and listen; but he had failed dismally. He had failed to do anything until he heard the words, "Now then".

The flight command kicked in and Ray started moving back. The man saw the boy move and pounced on him. He stopped dead in his tracks, before he could reach the boy and fell back. He started trying to crawl away from the boy using his behind.

"What, what are you?" he asked, fear written all over his face.

Ray was baffled as he saw the man change from his cool persona to a scared one. The man seemed to be looking past Ray, those eyes of his not so red anymore. He quickly got up and in an instance disappeared towards the kitchen. Ray heard the back door slam and he began to feel faint. Everything turned black and he fell, losing all consciousness before hitting the floor. The Tyler residence fell silent yet again.

Raymond Tyler woke up panting, searching his surroundings, his left eye crying. They were becoming more frequent; his dreams, his nightmares. He checked his phone, it was a few minutes before 3 AM; and there were a lot of messages too. Ever since he woke up in a hospital a week ago, Ray had not gone back to school; not that anyone expected him to. The doctors had told him he had had a shock and were going to keep him for a day for observation since he had not displayed any symptoms of PTSD immediately. Some detectives had visited him in his hospital room to ask a few questions, "Did you see the animal that attacked your mother, Mr Tyler? If so, what animal was it? There've been a lot of wild animal attacks in this district as of late, and right now we've narrowed the list to the cat family".

Ray had looked at the detective with confusion written all over his face, he continued, "It's alright. The doctors told us that it might be difficult for you to remember everything that happened that night, so we understand completely if you can't remember the beast. But we hoped..."

"I can't remember anything, I'm sorry."

"It's okay, Mr Tyler; if ever you do remember something, please let us know. Here's my card."

The detectives had left Ray still trying to fill in the blanks of the previous night. He had tried to remember clearly what had happened, but still, his memory remained just as hazy as it was when he woke up. He had been discharged and a therapist was recommended to him but he never went for any session. As he lay back on his bed, he knew he would not go back to sleep; and he desperately needed to sleep and not wake up. Ray had tried all his best to follow his father's teachings about staying strong; he had been strong this entire time, not once did he cry. He avoided the sitting room completely for a week, he avoided anything that would remind him of that night. If he could, without risking being sent to a loony house, Ray would have burnt the entire damn house just to try and forget. But he still had his sanity, so he opted to avoid every other room in the house except his own, the toilet and the kitchen. Today Ray did not want to wake up, he just did not have the strength to go to his mom's funeral.

*****

"What, what are you?" the man asked as he tried to crawl away.

He could not make out exactly what it is he was looking at but it was not human. He was used to being the hunter, the one who caused fear, whenever humans were involved. But in that moment, he felt what he knew so well from his victims: Fear; pure, concentrated fear. Fear of what he could not fully comprehend. His strength left him as he looked up at the almost transparent thing behind the boy. All had gone perfectly up until this point. Screw leaving a witness, consequences be damned, he had to think about his life at that moment. The being behind the boy didn't seem to be interested in leaving the boy and attack. This was his chance, he summoned the last reserves of his strength and got up as fast as his body could afford. He ran towards the kitchen hoping to find a way out; luck was still with him, he saw the backdoor and made his escape.

He kept running; all he wanted was to get as far away from that thing as possible. His first instinct was to flee from the country but he knew that would not be sufficient. The Society would find him no matter where he was, so he had to try and clear things out first. So he headed straight for the only place he knew he could find asylum. The bar was closed but he could hear voices, luck was still with him. Instinctively, he looked to see if he was followed or being watched, satisfied he was not; he ran to the back. He came into the cosy bar through the backdoor and stopped by the counter, disturbing the conversations that were taking place. Five people looked at him simultaneously. The barman quietly poured a scotch and slid the glass across the counter top, over to him. He took it down in one quick swig.

"One more please", he said breathlessly.

After downing his second glass, he quietly said, "I fucked up."

A beautiful lady, who looked like she was in her mid or late twenties, with emerald green eyes and curly blonde hair, who was seated alone at a table, looked up at him and said softly, "Speak."

"I did everything by the book, my lady, I promise. Everything! I couldn't have foreseen it, no one could, I swear!"

"Stop wasting my time and tell us what happened", the lady said, as she picked up her glass to sip.

He proceeded to tell them about his grand show; when he mentioned the almost transparent being, everyone stopped moving and simultaneously turned to look at him yet again.

"Are you sure that's what you saw?" a handsome brown eyed man in his mid-thirties, with black short hair asked coolly.

"Damn it Brad! I know what I saw, and it wasn't human okay!" he snapped.

"Watch your tone boy, you don't raise your voice when talking to me. Compris?" Brad said calmly.

"I'm sorry, I'm sorry. It's just that I'm scared man. I've never really seen anything like that, you know. Lady Estella, please forgive me, I know leaving a witness was stupid; but at least it was dark so he-"

"Shut up! There's nothing stopping me from killing you where you stand. Say one more stupid word and I will!" the emerald green eyed lady snapped. She stood up and walked over to the counter. She looked divine with her long red dress that hugged her body tightly, proclaiming her curves loud and clear. Her curly blonde hair bounced on her shoulders as she walked, her red heels making the only sound in the bar.

She gave the barman her empty glass, and without command he began making her another martini. She looked at Brad, her loyal handsome Brad, and softly said, "Could it be?"

"From his description, there's little doubt, my lady", Brad replied.

"So it begins huh?" she jeered.

"Estella, why would one appear now, especially besides a mere boy? Something just doesn't make sense here", a man in a black suit and white shirt said.

"Mr Andrews, please address her as Lady Estella", Brad said, eyeing him coldly.

"I don't belong to your house, dear Brad. My loyalties lie with my house and my master, and I don't even call him by any title", Andrews returned the gaze.

Both men stood up immediately. Estella found them amusing, their difference in character and everything. Curt Andrews, slim and tall, in his tailor-made sleek black suit; Brad, slightly muscular and average in height, in his black golf t-shirt and dark blue denims. She quickly said as they stood up, "It's alright, Brad. Andrews here, lacks the most basic etiquette anyone should be born with", and flashed the men her white, perfect teeth.

Andrews laughed a loud belly laugh as he sat down, "You've got yourself quite the pit bull here, Estella. You should learn to loosen up, man. Life is more fun when you do". Brad just looked at him and sat down as well.

"Listen, Andrews, I need you to look into that matter. I want a full report on the boy and all that takes place; hopefully, it's nothing. But if this idiot is telling the truth, it'll show itself again and we will confirm our suspicions. I wanna know how, in these dark times, a simple boy has such a powerful lamp with him. Think of this as payment for my house's hospitality and protection during your stay with us", Estella said, staring at her martini, "Have I ever told you, you make the best martinis, Hiroki?"

"Thank you, ma'am", the barman said as he bowed his head to Estella, who drank her martini with her eyes closed.

"Right, so you do believe this man's story huh?" Andrews said pointing at the still pale man, "But fine, if checking out the boy will make our houses even, then I'll do it".

"Will I be going with him, Lady Estella?"

"No, Brad, that won't be necessary. Curt can complete this task alone and he won't try anything funny, isn't that right Andrews?"

"Come now, Estella, you should give me more credit than that, of course I won't try anything. This is simple recon, I'll bring you back the info you asked for."

Estella smiled at Andrews then turned to the pale man, "As for you, the crime of leaving a witness cannot be forgiven, but since the circumstances you so claim, were unique; you will keep your head. That's the best mercy I can give you. So I, Lady Estella of the Eighth House; hereby banish you, Eiji Seto, forever from my House and the rest of my territory".

The pale Eiji became paler as he realised the magnitude of Estella's decision, "Please, my lady, don't ma-"

"If ever you are seen anywhere in this country, you shall be killed in any way possible. You no longer have the protection of my House and your many enemies will be aware of that by sunrise. You have until then, to leave my territory. You are now a vampire with no House and no master, may we never meet again", she then turned to Brad, "My blade please".

Brad handed Estella a curved knife with golden markings on one side of its silver blade and golden words-*'Per Mortem Omnia Coepi'*-written on the other side. The handle was of white wood with gold outlining patterns. It was a truly beautiful blade that looked just as sharp. She took it, and Eiji weakly approached her and exposed his neck. With the blade, she drew S curves on his neck that overlapped each other to- almost perfectly- shape the number eight, then she vertically crossed the symbol with one clean line.

"This is a blessed blade, as I'm sure you've felt. You won't fully heal from it, and you'll forever bear this mark for the rest of your pathetic existence. No House will take you in. The entire Society shall know of your status."

"No! Please, my lady, don't make me an expat. I have been faithful to you, Lady Estella, please! Our enemies will kill me, my lady, I beg you to reconsider", Mr Seto pleaded with his mistress as he began to kneel. A thin, sinister smile appeared on Estella's flawless face as she finally said in a sweet soft voice, "Best you get up and run, sunrise is a few hours away. There's plenty distance to cover and very little time to do it".
Eiji got up, his eyes glassy; and ran out of the bar.

"Well, that went well", a gentle voice said, breaking the silence that had fallen on the bar.

"Oh please, Risa, you of all people should know rules are rules. You were there when we made them", Estella replied the pretty lady, just about the same age as her, who was seated at the far end of the counter.

"I'm well aware of the gravity of the rules, Lady Estella, but you seem to have enjoyed yourself much more than one would expect. He was a valuable member of your House after all", said Risa in her ever so gentle voice

"Valuable, my left butt-cheek! He was a sick pervert, who's only real value was his slight resemblance to my brother, on simply being a master at torturing", Estella snapped.

"Do tell, where is that brother of yours?" Andrews cut in.

"I have many brothers, Curt, one of whom is your master. And anyways the details about my family that your master did not tell you, are none of your business!"

"Hey, hey, come now; I meant no harm", Andrews said in a mock apologetic tone, raising his hands up in surrender.

He knew the topic of lost family was a hot one, but he just enjoyed seeing Estella lose her cool; so he risked it for the biscuit, and boy was it worth it! Estella hated talking about her family, especially the only sibling she referred to as brother without using his name. They had been the best of siblings once, him and her, but events had taken place that could not be undone; and the rest is history. Estella found it sad that with the numerous siblings she had, the only people she considered her actual family were Risa and maybe Brad; Brad was relatively new, so she couldn't really say for sure yet. Risa, on the other hand, had been by her side for eons.

ASHTON R.M KHUMALO was born in 1999 and lives in Bulawayo, Zimbabwe. He enjoys travelling, reading novels and manga, binging anime and series, programming as well as web designing and development. **Divine Strings** is his first published story.

A DATE WITH DESTINY

Melissa M. Siziba

Groaning my way out of dreamland, I look around in frustration, secretly wishing it was all in my head. I feel very sleepy, and I wish I was little Tana right now who has absolutely nothing to worry about and hardly even knows what it truly means to be resident in this cruel world. He looks quite peaceful lying on his stomach, his face clear in my view and as always, his little frame almost taking up all the space. I just can't wait for him to grow up so that I can have this room all to myself, especially the bed because I have had enough of the daily kicks.

"Kudzi!" A female voice pierces my silent thoughts.

It's my mother, just when I thought it was all in my head. I quickly get off the bed and walk out, my curiosity exceeding my frustration. Mother never calls out for me this late, I hope it is not father again.

"Your father wants to talk to you," she says as soon as I emerge and my gaze locates the man before landing on the brown rounded clock stamped on the painted wall. It is a few minutes past midnight and I take it my poor mother has waited up for him like always. At least he doesn't look drunk this time.

"*Gara pasi*," he says politely, making me shiver from within.

He is unusually nice, and although he is my father, he is the being I fear most after God. Stealthily walking past him, I obey his command to sit, positioning myself very close to my mother and stare back at him. A blade can slice through the tension in this room.

"Since the holidays have started, I thought it would be nice to go somewhere as a family. I got two weeks leave from work and the day after tomorrow we will leave for Nyanga. You would love to see the Nyanga mountains, wouldn't you?"

I swallow hard and look at my smiling mother before giving a slight nod. He is unusually nice and it's making me nervous.

"You can go back to sleep now and tell Tana about it in the morning. Pack your bags too," he says, a slight smile playing on his lips.

I am only glad to get up and leave the room. I do not know what to think or how to feel. My father is never that nice. He even smiled at me! Maybe he has changed.... right? Maybe he is sorry for all that he has done to mother all these years and maybe God has finally answered my prayers. Closing the door and sliding back into the blankets I can't stop the smile creeping up to my face. My father smiled at me today! He is even taking us on a vacation, what could be more special than that? I mutter a prayer of gratitude before sliding back to dreamland, happiness being the only emotion I am feeling.

*****

Travel day is finally here and I feel so excited! My friends already know about it and I cannot wait to come back and tell them about the place. I have only but heard about the Nyanga mountains and the idea of actually travelling to see them still feels like a dream. We pack everything into the car then father drives out. I haven't seen my mother this happy in a long time and I can only thank God for it. This is the kind of family I have always prayed for. The kind of family I have longed to have and my father is finally giving it to me, it can only be God.

The journey is jovial and everyone is happy. I cannot remember a time when all of us were under one roof with happiness hovering over us. It still feels like I am dreaming and if I am dreaming, do not wake me up. We finally arrive and check into a fancy-looking motel. I am too exhausted to look around so I lie on the neatly spread bed while Tana sits next to me. I know he will fall asleep soon.

Just less than an hour into my slumber I hear them again. They are fighting. I turn and come face to face with Tanaka's innocent little face, his light snores a sign that he is enjoying his sleep in total contradiction to the chaos in the next room. I feel disappointed. A vacation to Nyanga was supposed to fix all this, wasn't it? So why are they fighting again? Silently, sure not to disturb sleeping Tana, I get off the bed. I do not want him to hear any of this, he is just a little boy. I carefully pace over to the wall, curious to hear what the fight is about this time. I am sure their noise is loud enough to disturb other guests in this motel but hey, I know they don't care.

"I told you she is nothing to me, we are just friends!" That's dad defending himself.

I have heard that statement over five times now, it seems they are fighting over the same woman again. I am sick of it. Who is she anyway?

"Your friend who sends you naked pictures? I am not stupid *wena* Thabiso! I am sick and tired of your lying games. In fact, what are we even doing here? I thought you wanted to fix things!"

"I want to fix things with the family, just give me a chance," he pleads again.

"How can you be so selfish and inconsiderate? You have a family for crying out loud! Your kids are in the next room. How will they take it if we separate? I am tired of this, I am tired of you! You are a lying, manipulative and cheating..." She doesn't finish her statement.

I heard the slap. That hot slap from father silenced her. There is silence in the room. For over a minute I am unable to hear anything but I know they are about to fight. It has happened before, the scar on father's left cheek is proof of it. I remember coming home from school to find him nursing the wound and mother was quick to hide the blood-stained knife. They were not expecting us that early but I saw it all, and pretended I didn't. I just took little Tana with me to change him out of his pre-school uniform and cheer him up, he was not supposed to see or hear any of it and I was determined to keep it that way. A thirteen-year-old already playing mother to her little brother you may think but that doesn't bother me one bit, it's always the circumstances that force us to grow. I stayed in our room with Tana silently anticipating the police to knock on the door, but they never came.

"I was stabbed by my wife." I pictured father saying but that was it, a mental picture that will stay like that. His ego would never allow him to utter such words and besides, he started it and I am sure mother got tired and defended herself. It had taken her over ten years to stand up for herself like that but why not just take us and leave? I am tired of witnessing these brutal fights, why doesn't she leave? Is it because she does not want us to grow up without a father? We can cope! The fights are killing me inside and my grades are constantly falling. I do not want my mother to do something she will regret one day; what if she kills him... or he kills her... what will happen to me and Tana? This is not my fight at all. I have to get out of here, I need space. I grab my jacket and gently shake Tana awake.

"I am coming just now, wear something warm, okay?" he nods and I walk out, straight into the next room.

They have started arguing again and it's getting louder by the minute. I slowly turn the knob, striving not to make a sound. I succeed and walk in. Mother is crying and father looks drunk. It smells like liquor but that was not the issue. Gazing around I find what I am looking for, the car keys thrown recklessly onto the leather couch. I grab them quickly and turn to leave. Did you see that? None of them noticed my presence. It happens almost all the time and I was expecting it anyway. As I close the door on my way out my gaze involuntarily falls on mother, her cheek looks swollen and her eyes are puffy. She doesn't have the strength to fight this time and it is written all over her face. She looks calm, painfully calm and that takes me down memory lane.

I was eight years old and I very much remember everything. It looks like a repeat of events, only this time I am older and outside the room. He had come home very drunk and beaten her to a pulp just because she had cooked plain *sadza* and veggies. She was a housewife, where was she supposed to get the money to buy meat from and besides, was it not his duty to buy it? The beer bottle in his hand, I remember it almost hitting me in the head. I probably wouldn't be here right now but I am. All thanks to the woman I am looking at right now. It hit her instead but she survived. The scar on her forehead is proof of it. I feel like running to her right now, I feel like taking her away but I can't, it's what she told me years after the beer bottle incident: "Never get in your father's way Kudzi, and if anything ever happens to me, take care of Tana *uyangizwa*?" I remember that statement word by word and I am abiding by it. Yes, I heard you mother.

I close the door and head back to our room to get Tana. We walk out of the motel, his hand holding onto mine for dear life. Maybe a drive will do us good. By the time we come back all will be well and the fight will be over. We get into the car and drive off. To where? I do not know. I just want us away from the chaos even for a single hour. I am thirteen, remember? Underage for a car license and probably one of the very few thirteen-year olds who can drive in Zimbabwe. As I speed down the lonely Nyanga road I pray we do not get caught. My mother will be angry if she finds out I went driving, one of the very few skills my father taught me.

"Where are we going Kudzi?" Tana asks, the belt stamping him tightly to the car seat. I look at the time, it is eight o'clock and I am very hungry. We had dozed off as soon as we checked into the motel, and lunch had been the last meal to grace our stomachs. They had ticked off on the first day of our vacation, who would be thinking about food at such a gruesome moment?

"Just a drive. Relax okay?"

He nods then looks out the window. The thunderous raindrops start bouncing off the car's roof followed by bolts of lightning. I feel scared, I have always been scared of lightning. What do I do now? The rain gets worse and so does the thunder and lightning. Tana looks scared but so am I. I regret ever stepping out of that motel, more so ever agreeing to this stupid vacation! I attempt stopping the car but I can't, my mind is all over and I am panicking. In that moment of fumbling, I somehow switch off the headlights and Tana instantly holds on to me tightly. My hands are all over and my brain goes blank, I cannot remember anything past that.

*****

I wake up to the blinding light of the ambulance I am being wheeled into. There are about four other cars whose owners I do not know. My head hurts and I cannot feel my feet. I look around for my parents but I can't see them. I notice a man scrolling on what looks like my phone and I conclude he is trying to call my parents. Wait, where is Tana? I struggle to lift my hand and tap one of the men pushing the stretcher I am lying on and when he looks at me, relief is written all over his face.

"She made it! At least one made it!" he says to the other man as they finally push me towards the back of the wide-open doors of the ambulance.

"Where is Tana?" I manage to whisper, searching the whole place with my eyes but can't settle on my brother.

"Tana!" I hear a familiar voice scream but I cannot sit up straight to trace the owner, everything hurts.

"Tana! Tana wake up! *Vuka*!" she screams.

It's my mother and a tear slides down, at least the fight is over now. I continue to hear her pitiful wailings from within the ambulance and the man next to me pats my shoulder. I want to cry but I cannot. I am full of indescribable emotions and I do not want to believe it.

"Where is Tana?"

I want to hear it from him.

"He... the little boy did not make it."

I felt like an arrow had pierced through my chest straight into my heart. The tears flow out, I cannot control them. My heart races, I am angry. But who am I angry at? I drove the car! I took Tana with me so it's my fault, right? I cannot control the thoughts flooding in and out of my head and eventually I scream. I want to get out of bed, I want to get Tana... but I cannot. I can't move my legs. The man is trying to calm me down but nothing is changing, it is all fruitless. From a distance, I feel the sting of a needle piercing my flesh then moments later I feel drowsy. I am slowly slipping out of consciousness. I pray I do not wake up because I have to go get Tana. He cannot live without me. I am determined not to wake up just like Tana, maybe, just maybe, mother will finally leave father, and go live a happy life. In case I find Tana, please remember that a girl like me once walked the soils of this earth and her name was Kudzai Kachena. A simple young black girl, who on the outskirts of Nyanga, Zimbabwe, had quite a memorable date, with destiny.

MELISSA M. SIZIBA was born and bred in Bulawayo, Zimbabwe. She is a Social Work student at the Women's University in Africa. Her passion for writing started in secondary school. **A date with destiny** is her first published story.

Facebook: Melissa: A tainted innocence.
Twitter: @that_zim_girl_mel
Booknet@NasheMel
Email: nashesiziba@gmail.com

DREAM MANIFESTATION

Sihlobo Bulala

She patiently watched the cheerful crowd continuously deepen their thunderous applause as a man of great stature, with a boldly chiselled body, drew closer to the stage. Finally stepping in front of the microphone, his hands brushed against his neat suit, and went forth to brush his tie as he regained his composure now that he was in the face of the many potential voters. The crowd, as though commanded by his very presence, lowered their high pitched tones and before long the space was quietly filled with curiosity.

"Ladies and gentleman", he began as he scanned the room, "It is with great disdain that we have to meet under such circumstances. It is saddening to note that today's world is filled with overwhelming and painful uncertainty, especially to our young women who have to live in fear of never watching the sun rise. But worry not; my candidacy is driven by a passion to uproot the evil that has grown within humanity. What you may not know is that I too have experienced the pain which comes with losing a loved one to violent behaviour perpetrated by people who by right should be protectors, the same way they would have pledged allegiance to their counterparts on their wedding vows. I was only ten years old when my mother died in the hands of my abusive father. Not too long after my mother's passing, my sister was abducted and I have since then lived my life wallowing in despair. I have spent all of my years replaying the possible events that could have happened and what I could have done to protect them. I'm a man who has lived in fear of the man I could turn out to be.

The world needs change, and I am committing myself to being at your disposal whenever you need me. I promise to be the change you wish to see, to be the leader who takes note of your pain and acts on your wishes, the leader who promises to stand with you in pain while investing in mechanisms that will help drive your pain away. Humanity is lost, but I am the leader who promises to do everything to maintain and encourage a civil way of life that will prove beneficial to all. We might not be of the same race, ethnicity or religious affiliation, but we will all have to compromise a part of ourselves to live in harmony. To achieve this, we all have to practice humane principles that will encourage us to live a free and enjoyable life in the company of one another.

Today I stand with the Art family. May the Lord be your comforter and give you strength to always lift your heads up".

The charming candidate continued to sweep the crowd off their feet with his heartfelt and warming words of comfort. As he trailed forth with his speech, her mind drove her back to the previous night's tragedy. A sharp pang grazed through her heart as she recalled how her mother's voice had called out to her as she suffered the torturous flames of the angry blaze.

'Lord curse the day I found love', she thought to herself in regret.

A part of her blamed herself for not protecting her family enough. Her soul hurt at the thought of how she had chased love over family. It ached that her last words to her mother had been awfully hurtful and she hadn't got the chance to sincerely apologise to her. On another note, her sister was nowhere to be found, while her father was held in custody and would soon be tried for committing arson. As she continuously drifted away from the crowd, she felt her soul lurch into a deep hole and wished that the earth could swallow her all at once. The pain was unbearable, and she felt like she had been set on a sulphurous fire.

In what felt like ages, she heard the crowd's cheers again, and when she lifted her head to catch sight of the handsome candidate, he had already left the stage. For a moment, she was clouded with a sense of regret as to why she had come to the rally in the first place. Political elections had always been the same to her, and she had come to understand that more often than not; politicians survived on principles whose footholds were based on blatant lies or half-truths. Propaganda had always been the ball passed in the playing field, and when a player got hold of it, they made sure to make a scandalous goal that pierced through the nets. Weirdly enough, for a change it seemed like the people of Atchtown had only good things to say about the candidate, but she was sure that only time would prove the truth of his character.

The crowd was beginning to disperse when she decided to look for the candidate, Mr Braun. While scanning the room, she picked on the crowd which had surrounded him and decided to play patient until he was finally free. She was in desperate need to know what would happen to her father. While she pursued the answers she needed, she knew that she was in denial.

She had studied the laws of the land well enough to know what happened to arsonists, rapists, and murderers. Having studied law as an international student in the United States of America, she had notably been the family's intelligent brains and it hurt that her family would no longer see her practice. They would no longer be witnesses of her great triumphs and most certainly would no longer be a part of her struggles.

She was about to step out into the open air, in defeat, when a voice called out to her. As she glanced back, she saw Mr Braun beckoning her to come over where he stood, as he seemingly waved goodbye to the gentleman he had been with.

"Miss Art", he forwarded his hand to greet her as she approached.

"Sir", she said softly and smiled wanly.

"I am so sorry for your loss, I hope you're keeping well. I was hoping to let you know that whatever you need, do not hesitate to shout. Your father was a great man, he stood for greater things", he gazed wistfully at her.

"Do you have a place to stay?" he asked.

"It is my mother I lost, unless you already forgot. Again, I'm the only Art family left, and I am in mourning, alone. Did your office have to hold a rally today of all days? You're feeding off of people's pain and you call yourself considerate? That's quite selfish of you." She was ready to spit venom as she realised that the more she drew closer to him, he wasn't as handsome and charming as she had thought.

"If I may find out, why are you talking of my father as though he were dead?"

She glared at him confused, her eyes dangerously boring into his.

"My dear, you might have lost your mother to death, but losing a parent to the judiciary system is equally painful. I did not mean to come out as abrasive, and I really hope that you will be strong during this difficult time. Should you need anything, I am a phone call away", he handed out his business card to her.

She starred at the card in disgust and quickly turned her back away as she started for the door. Her intuition was pressing hard on the belief that there was more than people were letting on. While she had spent her day falling deeply in love, her family had possibly had the most scaring day of their life, and there was no telling who was responsible for it.

She carefully trailed her way back home, avoiding the paths that led her to a number of people who were also seemingly scurrying to their respective homes. She felt her energy drain as she watched some high-spirited and vivacious young women chit-chatting; reminding her of the days she spent with her young sister. Not knowing what possibly happened to her slowly drove her to the abyss, and not knowing what to do about it scared the wits out of her. She was simply in a lost space, with no love nor hope for the future.

She was rushing home when suddenly she felt like she was being followed. Quickly, she glanced over her shoulders and as her intuition had guided her, an unrecognisable figure erupted from behind one of the trees along the pathway that now led to her non-existent home. Freezing to her bones, she came to a sudden halt and hoped that she would find something, a stick or whatever to protect herself.

"You're quite hard to be in touch with", a familiar voice spoke from behind her.

Sighing, she allowed herself to breathe freely as she tried to regain her confidence, but that also turned out to be a waste as her emotional turmoil seemed to have found a gateway to the outside world. Her tears poured down her face and she ran towards him, hoping that his embrace would numb her pain and make her forget all of her problems.

"I feel like I died and went to hell. I don't want to feel anything. I'm tired of being in this nightmare, and I miss all of them. It's all too hurting", she cried over his shoulder, and for a moment was thankful that she still had a shoulder to lean on.

"I need to do something to help my father. I feel like something is going on. That Mr Braun is dodgy, it wouldn't surprise me that all this was his doing. My father was a threat to his candidacy. Nothing really makes sense, and I need to figure out the missing piece", she drew back from his embrace, and wiped her tears.

"Are you sure? You really need to rest, let me take you home", her husband said candidly.

"I really need to do this. I'll find you at home. I feel like I need closure even though it won't get me the answers I need. I need to know what really happened to them. My father is in custody, and I need to see him before something happens to him. I need to find my sister too, I cannot bear the thought of what could have happened to her."

"I don't understand. How do you still want to offer help to the very same person who has cast this dark cloud upon you? Your father is a very powerful person, selfish too and it's possible he could have had something to do with this. You don't owe him anything", he sounded confused.

"As twisted as my father is, I won't leave him alone in a den full of blood thirsty lions. He has the resources to help find my sister, and that's what matters", she countered.

She had no reason to hate him for being adamant that his father had a hand in the destruction of the only home she had, but that's because he didn't know him as she did. While she admitted that her father had his own share of a twisted character, she knew that he respected life above everything else. More so, family was his pillar of strength and she was sure that he was as angered as she was by what had happened to the only family he had. Her father had easily become the most welcoming and accommodating man in their town, and for the fair share that he had been Mayor of Atchtown, he had made sure to deliver all of his promises.

The sun was about to set when she got to the site of the remains of what had previously been her home, a considerable safe space. As she wandered about the yard, her memory failed her as she vaguely recalled some of the details of her home. She tried to imagine which part of the box had previously been her mother's bedroom, the part of the room that had previously been her sister's artistic studio and it was with much pain that she realized that all of it had gone. Their once safe haven had been demolished by people whose humanity had been tainted by evil doing. It seemed as though it was now better to befriend animals than Man. At least one would know to tread carefully than to blindly drive into wolves dressed in sheep's skin.

The sky had slowly become enveloped by a dark cloud when she finally decided to pay her father a visit. If someone knew exactly what was going on, it had to be him, although as far as she was concerned, Mr Braun was a part of the circus that had everything to do with the amiss events that had blanketed the town since the start of the Mayoral elections. At first, just a few months ago, two candidates, Mr Swirth and Mr Shephered, who also happened to be friends, had been found dead in their car. The car had reportedly skidded across the road, killing one civilian before it rolled thrice and landed sideways a few metres along the road. Several weeks after that, another candidate was reportedly found dead in his office after suffering from a heart attack.

When she got to the police station, the guards on duty alarmingly stared at her as she went through the door to the server's desk.

"You can't just waltz in here. It's after hours. Visiting hours are over", one police officer said mockingly upon realizing who she was.

Ignoring him, she pleaded to see her father with the police officer who was at the front desk, emphasizing that it couldn't wait. Surprisingly, the officer beckoned her to follow him down the corridor until they reached the visitor's waiting room. In a giant's blink of an eye, her father came through, accompanied by a patrol officer who guided him to where she was. Seemingly disoriented as she had imagined, they warmly stared at each other as her father took a seat in front of her.

"Are you alright? What are you doing here?" he said, his voice showing concern.

"I need to know the truth of what really happened. I know it wasn't you, but I keep asking myself what it is that you did to make the people who did this to be this much vengeful. Whatever it is I'm certain Mr Braun is a part of it too", she tried to keep her tears from falling.

"I doubt Mr Braun knows anything. In fact he would be a fool not to watch his back because what's happening is bigger than any of us. If you have been following the news well, you should know about the new world order which most presidential leaders have been advocating for. The greatest tragedy is that the man who was in the opposing lane was found dead, shot in the middle of his eyes in his penthouse just a few weeks before the deaths of Mr Swirth and Shephered were recorded. He is the man who had been keeping the world civil. And now that they have eliminated him, they're free to do whatever they want", he stopped as he read her eyes, making sure that what he was saying was sinking in.

At this moment it had become windy and the sound of the swirling leaves was growing by the second.

"These people have yielded so much power that what they say goes, and a chaotic world is one goal they wish to achieve. They want to eliminate all authority within local communities so that they can control the world in its entirety. Darling, I'm sorry but I think that your husband is a part of it too. If he is not one of the benefactors then he's a pawn in the game. I would advise you not to go any closer to him", he was about to continue his lecture but something rather appalling happened.

His jaw dropped at the sight of a cuffed Mr Braun accompanied by a number of police officers, some of which were pushing him around like he was insignificant. He watched them surprisingly as they shoved him through the door that led to the cells.

"Your time is up", a police officer that had stood a few feet on guard behind him arrogantly called out, and in a few seconds he was shoved through the same door which Mr Braun had used a few minutes ago.

Unbelieving of what had just happened, she was left in a rather confused state and the information her father had shared had left her shell shocked. She couldn't imagine what would happen to the rest of the town in a few months and with the little knowledge she had, she decided to find out more about the operations of these powerful people. On the other hand, the thought that her husband could be a part of it made her tummy churn, and she suddenly felt uneasy. She wondered if that was the reason he had encouraged her not to try and save her father, or the reason why he had kept such a close eye on her. Now, she was no longer sure if the man who had recited beautiful vows to her six months ago had really loved her or it was all an act. Storming out of the prison, she swore that she would bite the bullet and shoot him in between his eyes the same way his circle had decided to have the world's superhero die.

Although she dragged herself home, she found herself drawing nearer by the second. She wasn't sure what would happen to her, but she was ready to have fate decide how her life would end. She was most certainly ready to meet the face of death if that's what it took to harvest answers out of her husband. As she drew closer, she realised that the lights were off and someone was roaming around the yard with a flashlight. Growing suspicious, she tried to hide in case there were more of them. In a split second he called out to the rest of the pack and shouted;

"She's not here. Come on, we will have to spread out. Make sure you bring her with you. I have no doubt you know what's at risk. She's to join her sister as soon as possible." The man roared, and all in lightning's speed they were moving out of the yard.

For a second, she had almost wished to surrender herself so she could be with her sister, but that too would have been in vain. Slowly coming out, she glanced around the area and charged towards the front door which was left ajar. As she stepped into the house, she screamed her lungs out as one of her legs drowned in a pool of blood while the other caused her to stumble upon a warm body. She fell on her knees, on top of the body's scared-looking face. She screamed in fear of what had befallen her. In as much as she had anticipated that she would find her husband in a somewhat queer state, she hadn't imagined that she would find his body lying helplessly by their front door.

She was still shaken and in shock when she heard a lowly audible voice calling out to her. Rising up, she tried as hard as she could to drive the body away from the path way so she could close the door in case the goons came back. Shaking her head to regain consciousness, she heard the voice calling out to her again, only now it was highly audible.

"Baby, baby. Wake up, you're having a nightmare", her husband's voice called out, and as she woke up she couldn't recognise her surroundings.

"Oh, thank God you're alive", she sighed in relief when she came to.

"Come on, try getting more sleep, it's a big day tomorrow", he said as he softly rubbed her back.

In a few hours, the beautiful morning woke her up and she couldn't hide her excitement about renewing their vows. Slowly waking up, she grazed through her husband's bedside and instead of feeling his body, she felt a crunched paper lying on top of his pillow. Fully becoming awake, she stretched the paper out and suddenly felt like she was short of breath.

The paper, covered in blood spots read:

Your husband died in the dream. THE NEW WORLD ORDER IS COMING!

SIHLOBO BULALA is a budding journalist who graduated with a bachelor's degree in Journalism and Media studies from the National University of Science and Technology (NUST) in 2020.
She is a content writer for URAFRICA (yoUaReAfrica), a Pan-African organisation, where she pens beautiful stories of Africa. She also free-lances for a Matabeleland South driven youth organisation, the Community Youth Development Trust (CYDT), whose aim is to enhance the participation of youths in developmental areas inclusive of local governance.

REBORN

Adrien Mapfumo

With the cover of night, he inconspicuously slithered into the room without anyone the wiser. In her raunchy, see through and lacy red lingerie, all that was left was for her to put on her black stiletto. Portia felt like she was on top of the world. She knew that the way she looked would have him drooling till kingdom come. As she was finishing up, she heard the bathroom door open ever so lightly.

"You couldn't wait, could you honey? I am yours forever now. Ravage me as you see fit", Portia said as she turned around with her eyes closed.

He placed a sensual peck on the luscious V of her breasts and she could feel herself moistening her knickers. A gentle tug on her lips raised some red flags and she opened her eyes to see a stranger in front of her. She was about to scream when a gloved hand covered her mouth.

"Beauty at its finest I see", he said, stroking her blonde hair.

With that he stuffed her mouth with a tattered cloth and plunged his ceramic blade deep within her chest. He was in awe of this moment, seeing that she did not writhe and how the light that had shone in her eyes dimmed.

Meanwhile, Zack was in the bedroom listening to music by Ed-Sheeran. Throughout his teenage-hood, his friends had always laughed at him for adhering to abstinence due to the no-sex-before-marriage notion. They always rubbed it in his face, telling him that "it's better to have lived and fucked than never having fucked at all", but the wait was going to be worth it. The honeymoon would be Zack's domain for each waking moment of his life.

He had it all figured out. Scented candles all around, rose petals scattered all over the bed and her favorite music playing in the background. Zack had Googled all he had to know in preparation for this day. He was ready to show his wife his sexual prowess. Everything was going according to plan until a masked figure entered the room, which made him jump and take on a defensive pose.

"I believe you have the wrong room, Sir. How can I help you?" asked Zack.

"If you must insist, your life would suffice", was the response.

With a tremulous voice he said, "What do you mean my life?"

"Don't say I did not ask nicely", said he, unearthing his blade and charging at Zack head on.

In that brief moment Zack was in a state of limbo knowing what the blood on the knife meant and that he was smack dead in a life and death situation. In a flash, he grabbed the bottle and whammed it straight into the intruder's skull, sending him heaving across the room.

Zombie-like, the intruder stood up and started towards his prey, playfully licking the blade's edge, which sent chills down Zack's spine. With the strength of a grizzly bear, he bulldozed the intruder onto the carpet resulting in a loud thud. Then he ran for the door, but as his flesh came into contact with the cold metallic handle, a sharp pain cut across his lower back, numbing his whole body. He could see his blood trickling to the floor, making a melody of sorts, followed by another jolt of pain which made him kneel. A quick glance behind him answered the whole debacle and down he went.

The intruder, Riley Murdock, stood atop his victim, contemplating his next move. Three minutes later he decided to collect the bedding and leave. With the linen sheets in hand, he removed his ski mask, pocketed it and simply waltzed out of the room. He then went to the trolleys where dirty laundry is deposited and threw the soiled linen in with the rest. After that he went about his day like it was any other Friday night.

The following morning, Keisha, who was part of the help at the Norton hotel, used her key card to enter room 55. Pigs do exist in this world but this one took the prize because it looked as though a whirlwind had passed through. The bedspread was missing so she went to check in the bathroom. Close to the door she came in, she could see traces of dry blood, with a trail that led to the bathroom paving way for her mind to run wild. She slowly opened the door and to her horror found a bleeding man wrapped in bath towels and a woman beside him, who had her eyes gouged out. All the cleaning utensils in her hands fell to the ground as she screamed at the top of her voice and ran back into the bedroom to call her supervisor.

Ten minutes later an ambulance and the police were on the scene. It was cordoned off to the general public with a few hotel guests trying to sneak a peek. Sergeant McKenzie was heading the investigation, saying that no one was to interfere. He was hoping that Zack O' Connell could give him some pointers but the paramedics had felt a faint pulse and sent him to the hospital.

"Miss Keisha, you are the one that found the body?" asked the Sergeant.

"Yes, I still don't believe what I saw", replied Keisha looking mortified.

"Do you know any of the victims?" he asked, jotting down some notes. "Is there anything you can tell me which may help us find the person responsible for this?"

"Unfortunately, nothing comes to mind. All I did was unwittingly find the poor souls and report it to hotel management."

"Why did you call your superiors first, instead of the police?"

"I wanted to make it clear to them that I was in no way responsible. Policemen are not reliable."

With a sigh, "Okay, you're free to go but make sure we can reach you at any time, so leave your contact information with one of my subordinates. By the way, do not plan any sudden trips too."

His partner Michael was standing in the doorway, lost in his own thoughts.

"Are you still with us, Mickey", he said, playfully snapping his fingers.

He was a chubby little fellow with beady eyes that could pry the truth out of anyone.

"Oh, it's you, talk about trying to give me a heart attack. You are still a thorn in my side I see", barked Michael.

"Well, there is no one like me that can cheer up that sagging face of yours", said McKenzie grinning.

"So, what is the list of charges here: B and E, attempted murder and 1st degree murder. Quite the rap sheet, if you ask me. Mickey we are getting too old for this and this case is really not up our alley. But we do know some up and coming investigators that are eager to make a name for themselves and would gladly take this case off our hands."

"Sergeant you must be joking. Don't tell me you mean those pompous fools!"

"Exactly! I know you hate their guts but the free time we will get out of this will be worth it. Camille did say you haven't been out on a date since you were promoted. This is your chance. On top of that the IPA (Integrated Police Agency) hasn't disappointed yet, has it?"

"Okay, now get on with it. You had me at 'Camille'. Call them already", Mickey said, looking away.

Giggling, "Sure thing Mickey, I'm certain they're going to be thrilled to hear my angelic voice."

At IPA headquarters:

The phone rings and the secretary picks it up. "Hello, this is IPA headquarters. With whom am I speaking to?"

"This is Sergeant Killian McKenzie from the Canterville Police Department. Could you please put me through to your Boss."

"Okay Sir, please hold", she said, calling upstairs. "Captain: old man Mac from the CPD is asking for you, he is on the other end of this line. Should I put him through?"

"I haven't heard from him in a while but put him through. This should be interesting."

The secretary did as she was told.

"Mac, I hope this is not one of those social calls. Didn't I tell you to call an ambulance the next time you couldn't get yourself to stand up because of that bad back of yours?" He said with a smirk on his face.

"Very funny Captain Fin. I assume that pun took you a whole year to prepare. I'm actually calling because I need your help. This is official business so I do not want any of your rookies. Just bring the best your firm can offer."

"You must have bit off more than you could chew. For the great Sergeant McKenzie to say that, the pride and joy of the police force. There is no shame in admitting it, but don't worry everyone knows we are the best."

"That smart mouth of yours will land you in my cell one of these days", said the sergeant.

"Okay, I'm sorry. Where and when do you want us?"

"Come to the Norton hotel right this instant."

Captain Roger Fin and his agency had set a record amongst their peers, being known to solve the unsolvable with each member handpicked by Fin himself. Kevin and Roy were to accompany him and hopefully they were going to help him close the case fast. Eager to get to work, they packed their necessities and drove to the Norton hotel. At the reception they were directed to the crime scene. On their way there, prying eyes were all around and they felt like they were on a tour in a haunted house. Upon arrival, Mac and Mickey said their goodbyes, leaving the IPA in control.

"What am I looking at?" asked the Captain.

"There are no signs of forced entry. Either the victim willingly let the assailant in or the perpetrator had his own key", stated Kevin.

"There is blood at the door, Roy take a sample."

"Before leaving, the old man had said the husband was found stabbed and lying on the bathroom floor. Meaning he was stabbed at this door and wiggled his way to the bathroom where he found the disfigured remains of his dear wife", voiced Kevin.

"In the bedroom, near the bed there was a scuffle. All is in disarray. Their arrangement of items beside the bed is a mirror image of each other. Two mahogany tables bear onyx lamps for those who prefer some night reading."

"We hear you but there is only one lamp that I see", stated McKenzie.

"Exactly my point, now let me finish. There was a struggle on the bed and one party hit the other with the lamp that is on the floor there, that person is right-handed but I shall conclude my prognosis at the hospital."

Everyone else had left the scene so they were depicting all this at first sight and they preferred it that way.

Fin smiling frivolously, "Are you sure you boys are not descendants of the great Sherlock Holmes because you never cease to amaze me."

"If only. Why would I be working at a shitty paying job if I were a Holmes?"

Seeing the devilish stare that Kevin was getting from the Captain, he quickly took back all he had said.

"Quit your yammering and move on to the bathroom."

The devil's playground it was. Blood all over the floor, a beautiful woman with hollowed out eyes lying on the floor. This was clearly the work of a heinous individual that apparently had something against women. It was a perversion in itself that the female was the main target and the male was collateral damage and just left there to die. Roy stated that there was no evidence of sexual trauma for she had no wounds in her nether region and he did not find any semen in or around her body.

The missing eyes were a cause for concern. Why would the culprit kill her and take her eyes? Lunacy not being an exact science, they ruled it off as the eyes being a trophy to the killer. Zack had put up quite a fight, so probability was high that they were looking for a male. The room was dusted for fingerprints but they all belonged to the husband, his wife and cleaning staff, which basically meant they had hit a dead end.

They were surrounded by clues which led them no closer to finding the person responsible. Solving this case was proving to be a mammoth task and thus Fin was wroth with himself for accepting the job. They decided to go back to the starting line. Before anything had happened, all was well until the perpetrator entered the room. The doors could either be opened from the inside by the tenant or from the outside using a key card. The only lead worth chasing down was the latter. The key cards that could open the doors of the hotel belonged to staff, being the housekeep, the mini bar keep and managers. With the suspect pool so large, they had their work cut out for them but of course the higher brass would never do such tedious tasks when the foot soldiers were present.

"The staff is all yours. Make sure they spill out their guts, and start with that Keisha. Roy she is yours, knowing Kevin he would daydream during the whole ordeal", said the captain as he went with the body to the Coroner's office for analysis.

The housekeep was interrogated; being asked about each of their whereabouts but nothing came of it. The Medical examiner had told them that Portia's time of death was between 8 and 9 pm the previous night so everyone was to provide an alibi for that period. With nothing coming of fruition, last but not least they went to the manager and he had a perfect alibi with a dozen witnesses. He gave them a gadget that registers all room entry involving a key card so they looked at the previous day's log. It showed that there was someone who entered Room 55 at quarter past 8 using a key card that belongs to the housekeeper.

When they confronted the staff with the new development, no one fessed up. This was a breakthrough but problematic still, for many of them had access to the card but no indication as to who it was. Immediately, they checked if the key card was still on hotel property and luckily it was. Roy and Kevin took the key card in question, dusted it for prints but alas, it was another brick wall.

Off they went to be by Fin's side at the hospital. Zack was stable, but seeing him on the hospital bed having undergone a lifesaving operation, it was clear that they were not going to hear from him that day. He was stabbed but all his vital organs were still intact. A few IPA members were called to babysit the bed ridden Zack until he awoke. The Captain then got a call from the coroner. They all listened as they were told that the fatal wound on her body was made by a blade with serrated edges.

It was established that it was not a conventional knife and it was probably homemade. But as for the eyes, a much more delicate blade was used, the edges of her cavity were not jagged but smooth. This was not the work of a surgeon or a person with medical expertise but it was still an impressive job. The coroner then said that the eyes were probably removed by a Swiss army knife and that a lot of care was taken upon removal. With all the information they had gathered it was still a dead end, so the IPA called it a day and went back to headquarters.

Like a phoenix rising from its ashes, Zack awoke from his deep slumber after a week of bed rest. The day after, the Sergeant paid him a visit to ask what he remembered. All he got were vague descriptions and his voice was so hoarse it sounded like two metal pieces scraping against each other. After that, Zack was allowed to go back home.

Being in a house where you were supposed to spend the rest of your life with the love of your life is horrendous indeed. Memories of all the time he had spent with Portia in that house crippled him. The following days were nothing but utter hell as he went through the painstakingly slow 5 stages of grief. Unfortunately for him, the second stage, that is "Anger" is where he lingered.

Riley had heard that Zack survived his ordeal but was heartbroken, so he decided to keep tabs on him for a couple of months. When he knew his routine down to the last second, he decided to pay him a surprise visit. One day when Zack came back from an evening church service, he found a hooded figure sitting on his couch, holding a mask. Upon recognition, his tears soaked the carpet as if a faucet had been opened and he knelt on the floor only managing to ask "Why did it have to be my Portia?"

Riley first read an old poem Zack had written:

The darkness calls to me every single day and yet I ignore it.
Deep down I know that it will one day consume me.

But I presume that when that day comes I will have the strength to face it.
A room full of people makes me want to claw at my flesh.
I curse as their mere presence makes me want to confess.
The demons that taunt me are lurking about, the day that I release them is the day that I please them.
Day in, day out, I think of suicide, the only thing stopping me is Heaven: I want to take a look inside.
I roam this Earth with the human race but I have never been part of it.
The reason why, is that I have never felt adequate.
In the shadows I reside, as everyone just sets me aside.
I am alive but I sometimes wonder what proof I have of that.
Could it be my birth?
Or the coming death record.
All I know is that the choice won't be of my own accord.

"I know all about you Zack, especially concerning your relationship. I bet you think she was still a virgin. She lied to you all those years. I had a list of all the people she had slept with and they numbered 10 whilst you were dating. She committed what I consider a cardinal sin. It is my duty to purge any and all that dishonour my God's wishes", was Riley's response.

This shook Zack to his core as the realization of the betrayal that befell him finally sunk in. He replied sobbing, "So, you are a heretic?"

"Not in the slightest. I could have left you as you were on that fateful day but I just had to see the face of the one I was saving. I am here today seeking your help to prune the scum of this world."

"I would never help the one that took my Portia away from me and just know that since I now know what you look like, I will hunt you down", Zack responded.

"I am a prophet seeking people worthy of his divine touch and I have a message for you. Our father knows that your whole life has been a façade, for day and night you dream of sex. It has been the driving force in your life, so when Portia died you felt cheated, for to consummate you had to find another partner. But I am here to tell you that you are no longer confined by that logic. Feel free to sleep with any woman you desire."

He felt as though his soul was bared for all to see, because all that was said touched him deeply.

Those hidden desires that we keep within us, thinking they are in a maximum-security prison can be released by one that is a master manipulator. All humans have the capacity to do evil deeds, but the choice to do good lies with us all. But because many try to conform to societal dictation, people do not show their core characters. A disciplined child is easily led astray because the influence of mob psychology has grown astoundingly over the last decade, thanks to social media.

In Zack's case, he was a wolf in sheep's clothing that had finally shed his false skin. Believing himself to be a sentient being, he was born anew and prowls the streets of Victoria Falls with Riley till this day...

ADRIEN MAPFUMO is currently pursuing a degree in metallurgical engineering, so knowing how things work fascinates him, especially when it comes to knowing what drives human beings to act the way they do. He is a Christian, so his main goal is to show readers that without the necessary mental strength to stand firm in the faith, everyone is capable of committing vile deeds.
He enjoys writing poems and reading thriller books by James Patterson, Tom Clancy and Jeffrey Deaver.

THE LAST LORRY FROM THE VALLEY
Onesmas Mudenda

This time I should be preparing lunch for my poor granny. Instead here I am, walking from fetching firewood in the mountains. Imagine if men were to see me at this time of the hour, and still not having started preparing lunch. Imagine how my aunt would scorn me!

'I wonder how your home will be. You are too lazy'.

She is the epitome of a good and hardworking wife. That is if I choose to believe her.

Last night I slept late. Can you imagine we had to sit still around the fireplace, long after the fire had died out! Granny was emotional as she told us the stories from the time of the war. In school, our teacher only taught us about the war that was fought by people that are far from our village. He never taught us about the guerrillas coming to my village, where they could be given a goat to carry and slaughter in the mountains where they stayed. Granny taught us all about that last night, though it was different from the other nights.

Last night it was not about the usual stories about the clever hare and the foolish baboon tricked again. Last night was more like a visit to the sad past. The sadness in the stories she told had me wondering whether it really happened in this village. Anyway, she proceeded to tell us after I convinced her to tell us more about the war.

She had protested, *"masamu alaamatwi muzukulu"*. That trees have ears and she did not want to risk her already exhausted life. I laughed at her and asked why she seems edgy whenever we ask about the history of the war. I have always told her that I'm now in secondary school where we learn history.

She told us about a certain young man that was killed by the soldiers for supposedly helping the freedom fighters. She narrated how one morning they came and just started beating him. They wanted him to confess to helping the guerrillas. The young man stood his ground as he bled profusely. When they realized that the young man would not sell out, the leader of the soldiers, a white man, commanded that he be made an example to the villagers. They shot to death the young man, tied him with a rope on to the helicopter and flew his dead body around the village. Can you imagine the dark cloud that covered the whole village that day? I can imagine what his family went through that day, especially his young wife and children.

Granny said that she could not help but ululate when the announcement of the end of war was made. It was something that everyone had long awaited. I asked granny what became of that young man that was killed and said nobody really knows. Our history teacher taught us about the Tomb of the Unknown Soldier at the National Heroes Acre. I think that young man rests together with other unknown heroes that perished during the war.

I explained to her about oral tradition and how it is her duty to teach us about our history. My history teacher is a very intelligent one, he always reminds us that we need to go to our grandparents and ask them about our history. He is young and smart; I doubt he is even married. He always comes by my granny's homestead, and she always gives him some relish.

Just two days ago, he came and gave her a packet of sugar, salt and a small bottle of cooking oil. She thanked him a lot for the groceries. She spoke his language and even jokingly offered him my hand in marriage. I laughed at him when he said he would not mind marrying me and taking me to the city with him to be his wife. I cooked porridge with tamarind; I remember very well he liked it.

They were not this close with granny when he first came to our village. I remember when he came in

January and our headmaster introduced him at the assembly point one morning, and said we should accord him the respect that we the Tonga people are known for. At the time, I had not paid my fees, so I knew that I was likely to stop going to school because our headmaster does not tolerate such nonsense.

If you do not pay your school fees, you better not show up at school. For if you do so, you will only be told to go back and tell your parents to give you the fees.

I had heard that he was stricter to us doing the first form. My cousin used to tell me that the headmaster's aim was to squash rebellion in its infancy, unlike others in form two, three or four who go and sit on the rocks with their boyfriends in the river or mountain until dismissal time.

This other day my history teacher visited me and granny. I was surprised but also happy to see him. He spoke his language and granny spoke back to him. I laughed at her and asked her when she learned that language. She told me how she had travelled to the city soon after independence. That is where she learnt the language. Ever since, they have been close, for she says he reminds her of the city. So sad she never went back once she got back to the village. I remember when he visited, I had been absent from school the whole previous week. So he came to tell me he had made inquiries on why I was missing school and was told that I had not paid school fees. So he went on to pay my school fees. I was happy to be back at school. Granny could not hold back her tears as she thanked him. That is how they started getting along and for the first time joked to him that she would even consider giving my hand in marriage to him for he had done something honourable, securing my future with school. Of course we laughed it off, again.

At last I am home; my neck was almost sinking into my shoulders because of the heavy firewood. Granny is not home, her *ndombonda*, the smoking pot is hanging in the shed. I remember, before I left to go fetch firewood, she told me she was going to visit her other grandchild who had just given birth at the clinic. I told her not to dare carry along her smoking pot for she was going to infect the baby with tuberculosis. Besides, the nurses were not going to allow her in with that nifty little smoking pot, let alone the bubbling sound that it makes every time she inhales was going to disturb the innocent little soul. She scorned me and asked how many people I know have contracted such a disease after using the smoking pot. She explained that it is one of the safest ways of smoking because it's of scientific ingenuity. Unlike the cigarettes, she always explains that the water inside eliminates much of the nicotine. I asked why she is always dry coughing if the science behind the smoking pot is unmatched globally. She claimed it was old age. I wonder why she felt compelled to leave it hanging there. Maybe it was because I had made an impression when I argued that it was going to affect the baby. Most of the time, I always lose the argument.

I wonder what the people next door are talking about. They seem to be gathered for some occasion, though there seem to be disagreements on what they are talking about. The one and only aunt of mine is there too. I can hear her voice.

I have to cook lunch now, *nsima* and okra will do. It is quicker to prepare. Besides I had bush meat last night. So okra will not be that bad. My history teacher might come in the evening. I will have to prepare a good meal for supper. I always do that. When he visits I always make sure I cook something nice. It wouldn't be fair to cook okra for him. He does not look like he would enjoy it. He is from the city, he is learned and to judge by the looks I doubt he would swallow a single morsel with okra. I do not want him to vomit. I always prepare something nice. I think fish will not be bad for him.

I know he loves chicken because almost every other week he buys one. He walks around in the village, after dismissal time looking for chicken to go and slaughter. Unfortunately we do not have electricity in my village, so there are no refrigerators. I guess he prepares it, and eats it in a day, or two days at most. I would like to assume sometimes it even goes bad and he throws it away. Can you imagine throwing away chicken meat?

After cooking my lunch, I will have to sleep. I will do my other chores later in the day. These days granny scorns me every time she finds me sleeping during the day. I cannot help it. Is it not natural for someone to sleep? Our science teacher taught us that when the body is tired, it needs to rest. The body will tell you that it is tired, therefore it needs to rest. Thus it will gradually make you fall asleep for it to regain its strength. I tried to explain to granny that it is due to the chores that I do at home. See, in the morning I woke up before the first cockcrow. I went to fetch water at the borehole. I hurried back home and by the time I was leaving again to go fetch firewood in the mountain, the sun was struggling to break free from the night.

Firewood is becoming scarcer these days, one has to walk long distances to the mountain to fetch a decent pile. For me, I cannot stand becoming a laughing stock in my village for fetching firewood just beyond the farms. I cannot be like other girls who are lazy, who gather small firewood that will not even outlast women eating their supper in the kitchen. A young woman should fetch decent firewood that can keep the whole family warm.

Anyway, doing all that obviously tires me. To granny, all that is a fallacy. She accuses me of being pregnant, always pointing at my breasts. She argues that I was not like this before. But I always stand my ground and tell her about science and puberty. Thus my body is developing fast as I approach proper womanhood. This started about a week ago when I was preparing chicken to cook, since my history teacher was coming over to see granny. I do not know why it happened but I felt like vomiting. I ran, leaving her to attend to the chicken. Anywhere the feeling went away just in time before he came. Granny does not want to let go of that incident. At every turn, she looks for an opportunity to always ask whether I am pregnant.

That reminds me of the other story that granny told me last night. How they lived happily along the Kasambabezi (only those who know the river very well bath in it), farming all year round and had fresh fish from the river. In the old days they had everything to eat. Unlike nowadays, when she has to wait for her son to send some groceries from the city. Back in the days, she always says they had everything there was to eat. That was until lorries streamed down to the valley, packed them without their consent, drove them across the dead plateau and dumped them in this drought stricken village. The last lorry from the valley met other villagers trying to find their way back into the valley. I wonder whether they made it. Granny thinks it was not a bad decision to go back, for the farms in the valley were more fertile than what she calls her farm now.

I explained to her that it is no longer Kasambabezi but Zambezi. She scorned me for not knowing that Zambezi is a meaningless corrupted version of Kasambabezi and that we should make sure that the name be rewritten back to Kasambabezi for the sake of our heritage. I always tell granny that it is not possible to do that. That name will only confuse the people world over. Can you imagine a white person coming from America or Britain, only to find that Zambezi is now Kasambabezi? They would bite themselves trying to pronounce that name. Why not just leave it like that, for the greater good?

Granny does not want to hear such a foolish argument. She always argues that tomorrow we will cry when they come and change our names to something meaningless. I always tell her no one will change my beautiful name. I love my name, Luyando. The only person that has gotten away with changing my name is my history teacher. He calls me Lulu. He says he loves my name. He even loved it more when I explained that it means love. He is the only person in the entire village that I have allowed to change my name. Anyone else who decides to call me Lulu or anything else, I ignore them, even not talking to them for the entire week. Some try to call me Lulu, especially big boys from school. When they write me letters, they sign off saying 'love you Lulu'. I do not reply such letters. Others go on to want to call me beautiful; they say because I am half white and close to an albino. I always turn them down. The only person who has called me beautiful is my history teacher because he means it. He is learned and knows what it means to love. Besides, the way he says it makes me feel something in me. Something that I cannot describe but when I think of it, it makes me to want to go back to his room at the school cottage, once again.

That must be granny talking next door. I wonder what the noise is all about. I can clearly hear my aunt too, talking. She is the loudest.

I had not even started the fire when I first heard granny's voice. That is what she always does when she comes back from her errands. She always camps at her friend's place and share old time stories. She always tells me about how as young girls back in the valley they used to play together. How back in the day they used to play with boys every time and their parents were never worried about them doing anything naughty because the month of July always came. That was the time when girls were taken to the river and checked whether they were still intact. She laughs when I tell her that nowadays it is not every young girl who loses their virginity like that. Besides, even from merely riding a bicycle I can lose my virginity. She always points out that nowadays if you leave a girl with a boy unattended, she will instantly fall pregnant.

Unlike back in the day, when it was a shame to be found not a virgin. It brought shame to the girl herself, her parents and the whole clan. It was a disappointment and it was embarrassing. As such, girls guarded their virginity with their lives. I always laugh when I ask her why they decided to guard what was between their legs but left their breasts out for all men to see. She argues that their breasts were an envy to everyone because they stood pointed straight ahead, unlike nowadays when young girls' breasts look as if they have breastfed already. I am quick at this point to tell her that our science teacher explained that breasts come in different sizes and shapes. So back in their days they were being unfair to those who had big breasts or saggy ones. Granny thinks that what our science teacher tells us is just an excuse and the truth is she might also be embarrassed by her breasts too.

I wonder what the argument is all about at the next door homestead. I cannot make out what they really are talking about but it seems to be a court like gathering. I wonder who the pregnant girl is this time. Nowadays, the girls are getting pregnant like it is a competition. I wonder why it is so. It disturbs, especially the girls from pursuing their studies. They seem to be heading this way now.

How anyone could be that heartless, I do not understand. For someone to just come and forcibly shove you into lorries, then dump you in a desert. An ancestral land, people forced off in a hurry. It is so sad granny went through this. One of the stories that she always tells me is how they were forcibly resettled from Kasambabezi. She always starts off with the lorries coming to take them away from their homestead. It had been months since the man-without-knees had come to announce that they had to be resettled. She retorts it was one of the saddest moments.

These people seem to be walking towards our homestead, and shouting. That's her voice, no one else but my aunt. She is the problem causer. Here we go, she is calling me. I wonder why she just cannot calmly call my name. She always shouts my name even without confirming what she would have heard about me. Like the other time when she overhead other girls talking about me dating the deputy head teacher of the nearby primary school. I had just finished washing my uniform and was in the process of rinsing it, when she bellowed behind my hut. Mind you, my history teacher was sitting in the shed with granny when she charged to where I was. I had quickly dismissed her antics as her usual hullabaloo. Little did I know that this time around she was really serious. She started howling her accusations at me, insulting me in the process.

"How can you date that old bag? Where is his innocence? With all the diseases that he has brought with him from college, he wants you to trade your innocence for that? Does he even know that you are still underage? Does he even know that he can be jailed for just asking you out?"

She then charged towards where granny was sitting with my history teacher. She had apparently thought she was sitting in the shade with the man that she had been insulting. She charged towards her and only cooled down after seeing my history teacher.

Why is she shouting again? She is already in our yard, and yet she is still shouting as if I am deaf? Here we go.

'Luyando! Are you pregnant?'
What does she mean?

'Hey, spare me the nonsense, have you been sleeping with that teacher that frequents here?'

'What...me? No...Aunt why would you say such a thing?'

I wonder how she has finally discovered.

Aunty is serious; she is now convinced that I am

pregnant. She checks my breasts, and inquires whether I missed my periods or not. I tell her I did, but did not think it was about me being pregnant. Our biology teacher explained that it is possible to miss periods.

So all this while, these women have been discussing about me. I wonder who told them I was in love with my history teacher. I told no one about him, but I have to admit, I really like my history teacher.

All this time, he has been visiting under the pretext of being friends with my granny. He always leaves in the morning, just before granny wakes up. We have done the lover's fight several times. Granny always goes to her hut early with her smoking pot, leaving the two of us talking around the fire place. We usually hear it bubbling into the night. The other time, she called from her room and asked who I was talking to. I told her that I was reading. I now wonder whether she had noticed something was going on between the two of us.

So I am leaving tonight with my history teacher, before anyone else in the village hears of my scandal. He has agreed to marry me. We are travelling to the city with the village head's lorry, the sole mode of transport to and from this village. In a few hours, everything has changed in my life. I do not know whether to be happy or be sad. My aunt said that life in the city is different from this cursed village.

She assured me she will be visiting me and my husband soon.

Born and bred in rural Binga, Matabeleland North, **ONESMAS MUDENDA** is a playwright and a linguistics student at the University of Zimbabwe. One of his drama books is a ZimSec A'Level set book, part of the study modules at Hillside Teachers' College and University of Zimbabwe. He writes both in English and Tonga. He looks forward to becoming a professional creative writer, and to also pursue writing for film.

BEWITCHED

Amanda Mpofu

I'm one of those many people that helplessly suffer from the syndrome of unevenly applying lotion on their bodies. Half the time, the soles of my feet, ankles, elbows and knees look as if dandruff flakes could fall from them. It doesn't help that I applied cooking oil because well, things are a bit rough.

Today is a very jolly day for me. I was called for an interview. Did you hear that? I am going for an interview; clad in my navy-blue high school skirt and this very shiny white blouse I borrowed from my mother. The shoes are a story for another day. You see with me, buying clothes is just a fantasy luxury. At 18, the festive euphoria that I suffer from is quite unique. That's because it's the only time I look forward to getting new clothes; the new skirt, blouse and pump shoes I always get! Now that I come to think of it, I haven't received Christmas clothes for the past two years. My mother will answer for it.

As I approach W.O.L.F, my heart starts showing off to the lungs and liver that like my brain, it also has a hold on my emotions. It's beating too fast, threatening to fly out of my chest. Pea-sized drops of sweat swim down my greasy face as I profusely rub my soft palms together. The way I am rubbing them is as if the generation of the next electrical units is solely dependent on me. I'm nervous! I desperately try to stop the sweat from trickling down my face by patting it off and slowly breathing in and out, but, something strange happens. A loud eardrum-crackling sound comes from somewhere between my granny panties and my place holders. I quickly look around to see if there are any fatalities because that indeed was a surprise attack. I too was taken aback. But I must say, I feel a whole lot better after that explosion. I feel light, like a huge burden has been lifted off my shoulders. Now I believe it when fundis say farting is therapeutic. Don't argue!

My knees get wobbly as I make it to the huge glass door in front of me. It automatically opens for me, so much to my marvel. I am flummoxed and feel highly honoured. I mean it's not every day that an ordinary looking girl like me has doors opening on their own just to appreciate her majestic presence. Or is it? Slowly I make my way to a huge shiny table a few feet away and there, a chihuahua is resident. You know those classy looking dogs with furs for years but looks for seconds? That is exactly how the lady seated on the table looks. Expensive clothes, a weave that looks like it cost an arm and a leg, and make up on point. Let me rephrase. Make-up on fleek! She is definitely not beautiful but she's one of those people that clean up so well you probably wouldn't pay much attention to her facial misrepresentation. Okay. Neither is she beautiful nor is she in between ugly and beautiful, but she's also not ugly. I don't know if it makes sense, but it makes sense to me, so I don't need to explain any further.

'Hello there, beautiful girl. Welcome to WORTHY OF LOVE FOUNDATION. How may I assist you?'

Oow she's nice. Well, she should be considering how she looks.

With a curt look at me and my garb, and a smile warmly plastered on her face, she attempts repeating the slogan in vernacular. I return the smile and abruptly cut her welcoming stint short with a polished,

'Good day, ma'am. I was called for an interview two days back, so here I am.'

I couldn't miss the perplexed look on her face. She dropped her jaw to the desk! At least she has nicely trimmed teeth. No. Nice is an understatement, she has perfect teeth.

'Uhmm well, welcome to W.O.L.F dear. Please give me your identification card while you, beautiful lady seat over there', she says, with her perfectly manicured index finger pointing to a fancy looking sofa. I heard these fancy people call them couches so I'll follow suit today.

One. If she thought using the full definition for I.D would make blood enter my heart through the medulla then she got another thing coming!

Two. I think she has a crush on me! I've been here for less than five minutes and she's already using endearments with me. I mean, she has called me beautiful, twice! Well maybe she's one of those girls that appreciates the beauty of another without necessarily being icy. I'm one of them too. Maybe it's part of her job description too.

My purse is not a pleasing sight, so I swiftly put my hand in my borrowed handbag and just drag it out without completely exposing its overused self. I hand the ID to her and quickly scurry to the directed destination.

I have never felt a seat so soft, I converse with my inner self.

You better get used to it girl! she claps back with enthusiastic zeal.

Just then I slightly lift my head to take in the appalled look on Ms Chihuahua's face. I'm not surprised! This is exactly what I expected. I go through it all the time when I'm forced to give someone my identification documents. However, I always feel somewhat confident when I must verbally identify myself.

That smile. She wants to call me but has no idea how to go about it. It's my name, that I'm sure of. It always threatens to dire up the soberness in one. It's mine after all, so what do I expect? In a moment she's right in front of me with that Aquafresh smile of hers.

'Please follow me dear,' she says and hands me back my I.D while giving me another one which she instructs to pin on my blouse just above my right 'breas.' I know what you are thinking. I'm saying 'breas' because my lady buns never fully developed, so why should they get the honour of being addressed with the full name when they themselves are not full? I have this strong and uneasy feeling that while my peers were called to collect the whole package, I was sleeping.

'Go straight to the 5th floor. The first room to your immediate left is where you will find the rest of your rivals. Good day.'

And just like that she turns, leaving me standing before a silver wall. Her designer heels softly knock on the floor, making the famous ko ko ko sound that I find myself humming the popular ko ko matswale song.

Wait. Why didn't I see that? I mean that watermelon shape just below her very tiny waist. It's so perfectly round, I find myself applauding the person that moulded it when she was little. Whoever it was did a completely splendid job. If it was an operating company and the person had been a contract worker, then they would have bagged a permanent job after such a marvellous job. Indeed I now understand how ecstatic and proud God must have felt when He looked at His creation and said, 'this is good.' Chichi has the full package of the perfect African body I tell you! With that crazy behind, her children will be the most blessed. I can already imagine a baby tightly strapped on her back comfortably seated on that plump pair! The wide handles on either of her sides are also just too perfect. I think.

My ungodly thoughts are disturbed by the opening shuttle in front of me. I think by pressing on those buttons over there, Chihuahua must have summoned it so I suppose I must get in and get whisked to the 5th floor.

I try my luck and step in absent-mindedly.

There are numbers on the wall of the shuttle. I guess I'm supposed to press five?

'Mommy, I need you right now,' I lament inwardly while tightly closing my eyes and loudly praying to the Lord to save me because this thing has just closed me in!

'Amen.'

Oh, there's someone in here.

The embarrassment on my face right now! Lord take me!

I'm not one to easily accept defeat so I mutter a begrudging and dramatic 'hallelujah' much to the amusement of the creature in here. He doesn't really laugh per se but twists his perfect mouth to the left like someone who has suffered a mild stroke. His looks are a sight for sore eyes but before I can take in all of him, a rich scent hits my nostrils. Had it not been too strong then it probably would have been sweet.

See there's nothing in this world that tames me like headaches. I have these really wild headaches that behave like a pregnant lady. Strong smells are a definite no-no. They make me sick to the pit of my stomach. I find myself tightly clutching at my nose for dear life. I can't get a headache today, especially not here. This man's cologne is way too strong for my feeble self. Up, down and sideways I take my eyes but there's no room for escape. We are completely closed in.

I think the creature noticed my discomfort so much he looks like a confused cockroach. No he's uncomfortable. Somewhere in his creature-mind he believes he's the one smelling. I'm saying this because I caught him trying to sniff at his armpits. What a funny sight!

As I'm about to bring him out of his misery and ask about the fifth floor, I hear a 'piiing' sound and the creature quickly scurries away.

Follow him, the inner goddess instructs.

I'm about to when the door of the shuttle slowly comes together and I yell a desperate 'heyyy, heyyy' but by the time he turns back to give me his attention, the doors have already closed.

'Please Lord save me. I don't want to die yet.'
I open my eyes to find no miracle. Again, I pray.

'Father God, please save me. I'm a good girl that's not ready to die yet. I'm still a vir...' and with that the doors open and I see the creature standing before me. See! Emotional blackmail does work on God. I just did it except I don't know what to say to this man before me. He's graduated from creature to man you see.

'Where to Miss?' the man asks with a barely audible voice while going down some stairs. The way he descends down them is quite questionable. So clean and extra careful it seems too dramatic for a testosterone pumped up person. Could it be that he's the copy of Adam that went missing in the exquisite garden?

I notice we are by the sixth floor judging by the humongous six written atop the staircase. This means we are heading down to the fifth floor. Okay.

'Going to the fifth floor, Sir.'
I want to look like I know where I'm headed.

'Okay', he says and adds coldly 'follow me.'
I do, ever so slowly and quietly.

There's something about the man right in front of me. He seems to be feigning a lot of masculine confidence and I must say it's working on me. He's scary and cold. In just a second, he's successfully added himself to my book of records where only a few people have been entered. It's those people that manage to bring out the coyness and the reserved person in me. I noticed I couldn't maintain eye contact with him and that's not a first. It's actually a second if not third but I think it's the sixt... Point is I can't really maintain eye contact to save my life though I speak ever so confidently and boldly.

'Fifth floor my lady,' he says with a 'frozen' curtsey and hurries off to what I presume is his office. He leaves me scanning his planky behind that's wrapped up in the tight pants he's wearing. Maybe they are the reason why he walks with unbending knees like he's on thin ice. I take in my surroundings and soon locate the room I was directed to. A knock once, twice and the third time, the door swings open. It is opened by one buffalo looking lady. I will leave it there. I greet and I get a 'dry cough' mmh from the three people occupying this room. Okay let me keep quiet.

One by one we are called for the interview, I think, until I'm the last one to go. The others went and came back to finish their snacks looking sour and now I'm nervous all over again. But what's difficult in talking about cleaning equipment? Beats me. I can't help but keep rubbing my palms on my lap because they are dripping wet. A whole respiration process just took place on my hands! The lady assigned to direct us to where the interviews are held comes and calls me. I swivel the place holders, where my buttocks were supposed to be and follow the lovely lady.

'Don't be nervous, girl. You will nail it.'

I look back. Oh she's talking to me. By the time I try to open my mouth to reply she's already knocking on a door. She opens and enters. Okay we are here. I summon my ancestors to work with me because I believe they are the reason why at 18 I'm settling for such a lousy job. A whole me working as a wall and floor engineer. It can't, so they better cooperate.

We are in. They are looking at me and so am I, zooming them. My eyes are darting across the room and I can't help but notice the mishaps that must have taken place in the maternal room when all the people in here were born. They are all facially disabled! Their faces display huge operation room errors, I repeat! Like this man to my immediate left; he has these horrified looking eyes. I think he was born through a Caesarean section and the first thing his eyes landed on was the good doctor carrying a pair of scissors. I think that's what traumatized him, the scissors. The evidence of his trauma, the enormous eyes.

Then there's this one with a round thing on his throat. I think his case is that of negligent nurses and doctors. While looking at him I make out that his mother must have passed out right after a torturous labour. The poor kid probably cried himself to a stupor in search of his milk he must have come across a stethoscope and swallowed it. Don't ask me how he did that but it's there, I can see it. It's bobbing up and down like an empty gourd on his throat. It's so fascinating how the stethoscope keeps vibrating when he gulps down that tea. I freeze. I lift my head a bit to find everyone looking at me. I must have laughed out loud while staring at that tourist attraction feature on that sausage-like throat.

'Miss Liquor, if you can please be attentive. This is no circus.'

The sarcasm!

It's a lady with scrawny locks. I don't know why but I thought to myself that I'll never eat mopane worms for the rest of my life after taking in the contents on her head. This lady here has a permanent surprised look on her rough contoured face. I think she's a rumour and gossip monger too, judging by the shape of her mouth. It's turned downwards like the small letter n. She looks at me with an attitude. I get it. I'm beautiful, if I must say so myself. My complexion, my smooth spotless face and my tiny pink lips are my favourite features. You know this colour that you get when you make tea without enough milk? That dull boring brown colour you get after making very strong black tea and you pour it in an empty cremora pack and shake just so you can get a milky taste on your beverage? My skin colour is exactly like that. It's actually a perfect colour for the skin, not the tea.

'So Miss uhmm, please tell us about your name.'

'Not that my name has anything to do with this interview but it was a spelling error, I guess.' I mumble the last part. My name depresses me. That white registrar did a number on me. I'll have to see a therapist one day if people continue reacting this way all the time.

'Here, take this,' the Jah Lady says with an attitude.

It's a container of Vaseline. Did I tell you about my syndrome? I guess the lady just noticed my white knees and elbows. I stand up, take the container, open it and scoop a fingertip full of its contents and apply on the hotspots. I can see that the people here are appalled by my actions, but do I care? Not at all. I continue with my 'operation apply lotion' and when I'm done, I put the container in my handbag and take my seat. The lady has her hand extended towards me but I bluntly ignore it. The Vaseline is now mine. This is my manna from heaven. No more Roil on my skin!

'What is a young, beautiful, 18-year-old with 8As and 13 points doing at a cleaners' interview? Shouldn't you be in varsity?' Stethoscope asks with a heavily concerned look on his face.

I choose to look anywhere but at his pipey throat while he's speaking. At least when he's quiet the apparatus on his throat becomes steady.

'I wouldn't be here if life had favoured me, Sir. At least it threw me grapes and now I'm making wine out of them,' I reply nonchalantly.

They are surprised. They didn't except this. Neither did I. The words just rolled out of my mouth before I could do anything. To avoid any negativity I quickly add, 'I'm Likhwa and I think I'm bewitched.'

"Nothing comes out of nothing" is a mantra that **AMANDA MPOFU** feeds on to find strength and determination to face her everyday challenges head on. At 23, she is a final year student at Midlands State University pursuing a BSc Honors Degree in Psychology. Born and bred in Bulawayo, Zimbabwe, Amanda has scribbled many enticing unpublished short stories and poems. She draws inspiration from her late grandfather, Mr G Mpofu, and her high school literature teacher, Mr Pentecost Mate, who she considers fundis by default. Her long term goals include being a globally celebrated mental health activist and a renowned author.

mandaziyambi@gmail.com
mandyammanda- Instagram
Mandy Amanda- Facebook

TEMPERING WITH THE JEWELS
Shylet Majoni

She was running in the forest. She ran as fast as she could but whatever was chasing her was closing in. Suddenly she saw an odd house; it was good enough to be a refuge. She bolted towards it, opened the door and closed it behind her. She locked the door then pushed the table that was in the middle of the room, fixing it against the door to prevent the intruder from entering. That happened in a blink of an eye. She was safe from the intruder. She turned back to look for something that could help her. Oh oh! She was the intruder. A group of ten girls was standing behind her, all of them aged between 15 to 19 and an old woman was sitting on a rocking chair on the far end of the room. She seemed blind to everything, or she was really blind.

There was a loud bang on the door.

"Open the door you stupid bitch!" a voice from a man outside said.

He was shouting and kicking the wooden door. The table she had pushed against the door was bouncing back and forth. The bang grew louder; the teenage girls looked at her without blinking. It was creepy. One of them mumbled something but she couldn't hear the words properly. Suddenly the bang became softer, and the voice turned into a woman's. She recognised it, it was her mother.

"Lethue wake up, you will be late for school," she called from outside the room.

She opened her eyes, she had been dreaming again, the same dream. She had been having this dream for the past three weeks. Except it changed a bit every time, a new detail or feature was added every night. Three days back she woke up before the girls, yesterday the girls appeared and today one of the girls said something, something she didn't hear clearly.

"I'm sure I will hear the words properly tonight," she said to herself.

This was becoming normal to her, like someone was telling her a story, kind of a treasure hunt. Every night she went to bed expecting to have the dream and it never disappointed. It came as expected and with new details, new leads, revelations and clues. But to what? She had told her mother about the dream but she had said dreams were too useless to focus on. This was something important though, at least to her it was. It must have a meaning or reason. Why would she dream the same thing time and again?

"I'm coming, mom."

She quickly got into the shower and eight minutes later she joined the family in the kitchen. Everyone was getting ready to leave the house, except for her father who was still in his morning gown, reading a local newspaper that had just been delivered. He had nowhere to go. Her father, Mr. Paulos Hlatshwayo, or "Bra P" as they called him in the streets was a decorated detective in the police force. He had been recently suspended over a case that implicated him in a drug deal where 4 boys overdosed and died. Three Dlamini brothers aged 17, 19 and 23 as well as their 15 year old cousin, died claiming they had bought the drugs from Bra P's patrol car. The cousin, who died two days later at the hospital, identified Mr Hlatshwayo as the seller and also the driver of the car. He was suspended and placed under investigation. Mr Hlatshwayo had an alibi that checked out. He was not on duty that night and the vehicle number stated by the boy was parked at the garage all night, CCTV had a record of all that. It was all going good for him, it seemed as if he was being framed. His lawyers had also argued that the boy gave the details while high on drugs.

Lethue's mother, Sibongile Hlatshwayo, a teacher and mother of three girls and one boy; Lethubuhle aged 19, Dalubuhle (boy) aged 16 and the twins Sinenhlanhla and Nonhlanhla aged 14. Sibongile was a hardworking woman and she raised her kids very well. She believed in spoiling them. They had everything they needed and anything they asked for, she would provide.

"Anything about you today dad?" Lethue asks.

"Yea, the usual. I don't think the Dlaminis will believe that I am innocent even if the judges say so. They really believe I killed their boys with those drugs," he pauses. "They are talking to every news outlet and the more I read their story on the papers I get convinced that I might be the guy they claim they bought the drugs from."

He laughs a bit.

"Well then you need to stop reading those newspapers, Paul," her mother intervened.

"Enough with all that case update, let's finish our breakfast and rush to school."

Lethue's phone vibrates. There are nine new messages and five missed calls. She skims through the messages, nothing important, just random boys hitting on her. All the calls were from her best friend Amara. She calls her back:

"Girl, what's wrong with you? Why are you not picking your phone," Amara's first response without greeting.

"Hi Lethue, how was your night? Ooh! Hi besty," Lethue says sarcastically.

"I cannot ask you that, you are going to start with that dream thing of yours. Listen, I sent you an audio. DJ Ray just dropped a new hit on gender based violence and drug abuse. Listen to it. He has this campaign of his that will bring awareness. It's a big project. We will talk about it at school."

Just like that, Amara hung up.

Gender based violence, yes that's a thing but drug abuse. That won't work, considering my dad's case right now.

She listened to the song and loved the lyrics. The song had a strong message and as creative as she was, she started having ideas of how she could save her father using the DJ's awareness campaign.

*****

"That's your dad," the young girl said.

"Please save us, save us, he will kill us," they all chorused.

They started pulling her down, the banging was loud and the girls' pleading was annoying.

"Get away from me!" she screamed and immediately woke up.

She usually woke up from her dream at dawn, but it seems this time the dream had come earlier. It was 2:25 in the morning. She sat on her bed, troubled by the dream. She finally heard the girl's words "That's your dad".

What does it mean? Is it in connection with the Dlaminis? But they were boys and my dad would never be this aggressive.

"Save us, he will kill us," they had pleaded.

This was all confusing.

Later in the day she tried telling Amara about the dream and the girls but her best friend seemed to have more serious issues to discuss.

"Girl, here is how this will go. This weekend we will have a march from school to the city square with DJ Ray, he will perform a few songs and a few of us will share messages on GBV and drug abuse. From there, we will go for a video shoot for his new hit single at the cooler House Lake," Amara said with enthusiasm. Lethue knew enough not to try to change back the subject to her dream issue.

"I cannot participate in this Amara, you know my dad..."

"I know but if people see you in that campaign it might help," Amara interrupted her.

"I have a speech," Lethue said.

"That's my girl, I will tell Ray."

"I never knew you were close with Ray."

"Well, we weren't. My neighbour introduced me to him. She is in Ray's crew, make-up thingy."

"Oh! Fadzayi, right?" Lethue asked, raising her eyebrows.

"Yes that's her, let me run girl. I will see you tomorrow at school, got a lot to prepare. Work on that speech of yours."

Lethue had always wondered if her friend cared about her at all. Every time they spoke, it seemed as if everything was about Amara, whenever she had something to say or something that bothered her, Amara would wave it off. Even when she tried to talk about their friendship being one-sided, the same thing happened.

The Dlaminis had set up a press conference and invited all media houses to talk about how unfair it was for them that all their sons were dead while their killer was walking free with a possibility of winning the case at court. Lethue pulled up her hoodie and joined the small group of people that was gathered at the press conference. The sight of the boys' parents was sad. Their mother was wearing traditional black grieving clothes.

Culture requires those to be worn by a widow who just lost her husband, why is she wearing that? Lethue thought. She realised how wrong it was to criticize her and she quickly turned her focus to what was being said.

"....He sold drugs to teenagers, his job is to remove drug dealers off the streets but it turns out he is the drug dealer. On Monday the court will decide his case. We invite you to rally with us and demand justice for our boys," Mr Dlamini said.

It was impossible to stand there and not judge, Lethue saw all that as a charade. They wanted people to feel sorry for them and help them call for the sentencing of an innocent man and call it justice. She soon realised that she was being judgey again so she left.

Her father was the sweetest man she had ever known. He was kind, loving and gentle. He would never do anything to harm a child. To her, Mr Paul Hlatshwayo was a superhero. This city was supposed to be thanking and honouring him, instead of accusing him of being a criminal. She wondered how the newspapers that had written countless articles about his heroic arrests; how he saved the day a multiple times, busting criminals, recovering stolen goods and making people happy, could turn around and write badly about him. How could they not see through this lie from the Dlaminis? At school everyone was pointing fingers at her. She could hear whispers about her dad, drugs, killing boys and Dlaminis. It was affecting her social life, some students had even submitted a petition to the headmaster demanding her removal from being the school deputy head girl. She always found strength in her mother. Once, she requested to be transferred to another school but her mother refused.

"You must learn from this Lethue, do not run from it, face it. I am here with you and we are going to face it together. Your father will be cleared of these charges and the lessons we will get from it will be a treasure."

Lethue thought hard on these words as she wrote the speech. She wanted it to be a loud speech that would free her father, free her family and free her from this dark cloud. She listened to DJ Ray's song as she wrote her speech, it was just as she wanted it to be.

The weekend came and everyone was in high spirits. DJ Ray was a popular figure; a very handsome man in his early thirties. Kids loved him, especially young girls who were crazy about his looks. The turn up that day was amazing. School kids from the local and neighbouring schools had come to stand up against gender based violence and drug abuse. They had placards and banners written all sorts of messages that denounced the menace. Police escorts were out in full force. The event was a resounding success. Never in the history of the city had an event of this kind been organized.

At the city square, the school pupils were joined by a large crowd of parents. Ray stepped on the stage and the whole square went crazy. He was a very vibrant performer and his music related to both young and old. His influence was very wide, he had groomed a lot of young people in the country: Singers, dancers, producers and the likes.

There were various speakers lined up that day. Lethue had heard that Mr Dlamini wanted to be part of it but Amara told the planners to reject him, something good that her friend had done for her in a long time. She stood there listening to the speakers. Their stories were painful; women beaten, mothers whose kids were abducted or murdered, a relative who lost someone to drugs. Lethue wondered what had happened to the world. Who rapes and kills a 12 year old girl? Where are all those young women who have been disappearing with no trail? She remembered her dream and cringed. Could it be true that her father is a human trafficker and drug dealer?

"That's your dad," the young girl had said referring to a man who was violently banging the door, calling her a bitch.

But he is my father, she thought to herself. *He loves me, a young girl, how can he hurt someone else's young girl when he has a young girl child himself?*

"That's you, girl", Amara said, giving her a nudge on the shoulder.

She quickly snapped back to reality. She was being called to the stand. There was an awkward silence, people were probably thinking: *Her father is being accused of drug dealing, how can she participate in an anti-drug abuse campaign?*

She wanted to give this speech. She had taken all her time preparing it. This is why amid the awkward silence that could have given her cold feet, she pressed forward until she was in front of everyone. The stage was beautiful, well decorated and way above everyone. She looked at the crowd that was silent beneath her, as if they were waiting for her to say all the wrong things and then stone her. She rolled out her paper, placed it on the pulpit, took a glance at the crowd once more and she thought.

This speech will not do any good here, she rolled it back and removed the microphone from the stand. Her public speaking skills kicked in. If ever there was a moment to prove that her father was not a drug dealer, this was it. It was now or never.

*****

Detective Paulos Hlatshwayo had made it to the headlines. His story was on the front pages of every newspaper. **'CLEARED OF ALL CHARGES.'** Some claimed his daughter's speech contributed to the victory. Lethubuhle had said all the right things during the weekend at DJ Ray's campaign, even the Dlaminis themselves started questioning their stand. They cancelled the demonstration they had called for at the courthouse. Asked for the reason for cancelling, they simply said, "We trust justice will prevail in the court, we will accept whatever decision."

The problem was Lethue was not back yet from Ray's video shoot. They were supposed to be back on

Sunday, Bra P was cleared on Monday and now it was Tuesday. Last time they heard of her was when they called Ray's PA on Sunday. She advised them that everyone who was on the shooting list would be delivered at their homes on Monday morning. Now that assistant's number was offline.

Detective Hlatshwayo was reinstated on Wednesday. On his first day back at work, he had to deal with 13 cases of parents who were reporting their children missing. Their kids had gone on a video shoot with DJ Ray during the weekend, they were supposed to be back on Sunday evening, they had lost contact with the team on Monday. Now it dawned on the detective that his child was missing, probably-abducted. He blamed himself for being too reluctant on the case. How can his child be away from home for a week and he doesn't even trouble himself?

"Parents are reporting their kids missing," Paulos says.

"What parents?" Sibongile replies.

"Parents of the kids who left with that DJ, the video shoot where Lethue went."

"Paul, is this another kidnapping case? You mean she was taken by traffickers?"

He did not know how to reply to that, he wasn't sure, but that's what he thought too.

"We are going to the DJ's house, I will keep you posted."

Ray and his team knew nothing about the missing girls.

"Are you sure these girls were not in your team?" Detective Sibanda asks.

"100% sure, Sir. We had 14 girls and 8 boys on our team, all their parents signed indemnity forms and the kids were returned home safe on Sunday evening. Our bus delivered them at their doorsteps," a bald cute lady replies. She was Ray's assistant.

They took both Ray and his team in for questioning. They knew about Lethue's speech but she was not part of the video shoot team. All the missing girls were not on the list. Amara was on the list. Hlatshwayo knew she was Lethue's best friend so he called her in for questioning. She denied any knowledge of Lethue being part of the video shoot crew.

"All I knew was that she was going to give a speech at the campaign sir. She never signed up for the shoot, I never asked her to, because I knew she didn't like these things."

Something was fishy but Hlatshwayo believed her. That night his wife cried painfully. They both knew that the possibility of finding Lethue was slim, girls who disappeared were never found.

*****

Lethue woke up in a small, overcrowded, dirty and smelly room. There were more than fifty girls there. She remembered getting on a bus. Amara was not in it. They were told that the bus was heading to the video shoot venue. She remembers a commotion when they realised that it was taking a wrong route. She remembers the driver and his assistant putting on masks, a strong choking smell in the bus and then nothing. How they got here, where and when, she had no idea. The other girls were bundled in small groups. Some were crying while some were trying to be strong, not because they had strength but because there was no hope in doing anything, even in crying. It seemed they had been there longer than her.

"We heard the other men fussing over you. They said you are some policeman's daughter. Do you think he can save us?" one of the girls who looked older than all of them asked. A second glance at her would tell you that she is young but being at this place has ruined her looks. They looked like abandoned precious treasures, like rusting gold vessels. Someone was messing with the jewels.

*****

"There must be another way Bra P", Detective Sibanda says.

"It's the only way bro. How will I face my wife if our child dies? Even if we save her, those thugs will implicate us, they took my daughter Sibs! They knew she was my daughter and they took her. They are onto us."

"But still, it doesn't have to go down this way. You can disappear, we can make you disappear, you can start a new life somewhere else."

"And continue with this, Sibanda? The Dlamini boys' case got me thinking: how many bad things have we done and got away with? We are hurting people, we have to stop. I am getting off like this, I hope you find a better way of stopping yourself. Just save my daughter."

The following day detective Hlatshwayo was found hanging in his office. There was a note on his desk which read: *THEY ARE AT 1416 TOLL HOUSE, SAVE MY DAUGHTER.*

Detective Sibanda led a raid at the address and they found all the girls. Lethue had read of such rescues. Her father was lead in most of them, she had seen pictures of him holding the girls in his arms after saving them. When she heard the police exchanging fire with their captors, she knew this was her day to be rescued by her superhero. She remembered the dream "It's your dad", the girls had said. *Yes it's my dad*, she thought to herself, *except he is not shouting at us, he is the saviour*.

SHYLET MAJONI was born and bred in Bulawayo, Zimbabwe. She is an Archaeology and Museum student at the Midlands State University. She enjoys travelling.

HOME

Linda Masudze

The last weekend of the month found her sitting alone on the balcony of her apartment. Mudiwa had called in after his dramatic departure and said he would be going to Cape Town for a week to attend a workshop. They both knew it was a lie. Contrary to her expectations, he did not ask about the baby. That broke her heart. Who had thought that the birth of something so beautiful would mark the end of their bond? God! Was she meant to do this alone?

What went wrong, my love? Your heart was supposed to melt at the mention of the news. You should have hugged me and assured me. That you will never leave. And that you will protect us. Fight for us. Be with us. But you left. And now what will I tell my child? That your daddy didn't want you? Or maybe you are dead or in some faraway country? What explanation will I give for your absence? Tell me! How can you be so selfish? Why must it always be about you? Why must an innocent soul be condemned to such? My poor baby! When your tiny friends talk about their daddies, what will you say? I am sorry it had to be like this. Now I am alone. I will sing you a birthday song alone. When you are sick, I will stay up all night alone. I will be there for you alone.

When they tell the story to their grandkids they start with the boutique incident.

"He looked rich," Christine laughs. "And kind too. My bank card had declined so when he offered to pay for my shoes, I died with embarrassment but said yes nonetheless. You see, he always thought everything could be solved with money."

Time went by, months even and they saw each other again. It was at that same boutique. This time Christine offered to pay for him also and that is when they went on to spend the next three Christmases together until a slight change in plans occurred, as Mudiwa likes to put it.

Mudiwa had just gone out with a couple of guys to a club and his mother followed him there with the tragic news. At age forty-four, Thando, Mudiwa`s mother had learnt the secret of looking ten years younger without losing a sweat. Young hot blooded men still whistled when she passed by. On this particular night she wore a slim fit winter jacket, yellow in colour with matching heels and a black dress. As soon as she saw her son, she ran over to him and cried, "He is in the hospital!"

"Who?" Mudiwa asked nerve stricken.

His mind was already perplexed by the sight of his mother weeping gravely at a club! For goodness sake! He cringed at the thought of all the theories an onlooker might have come up with. How many young men can testify that their mothers follow them to the club and summon them whilst four feet under dancing to the latest Migos or Nasty C? Onlookers' theory might be well this wailing lady in yellow is into gigolos and this particular one has broken her aging heart. LOL.

Onlooker theory number two might be: well this guy is the grieving lady's son who stole her money and is now making it rain in the club with his mother`s money. LOL.

"Your father is in the hospital, Mudiwa!" Thando explained, trying hard to contain herself.

"But you are my father, mom. What are you talking about?" Mudiwa laughed gaily taking her into his arms gently. He then continued to laugh at himself for thinking that something serious had happened.

Thando forcefully pulled her tiny frame away from him and her small eyes shot daringly into his. The truth then dawned into the son's mind. After a whole twenty six years Thando still loved the man who abandoned them for another woman. Yet she still loved him. The urgency in her voice, the pleading in her tears and the violent way her body was shaking were all testament to the fact. What could she possibly still see in that undignified human being? He left them with nothing. Literally gave them the middle finger and here was Thando begging the unwanted son to go see him on his deathbed.

"He was involved in an accident and lost a lot of blood. He needs a transfusion but they can't get any from the blood bank. You need to go right now and see if you can help him. You are O Positive and so is your father."

"I don't know who you are talking about. I only have one daddy and I am looking at her right now. She looks fine and healthy. I love you her much to see her out here in the cold talking about some strange man I have no relationship with."

Thando looked at him in disbelief, and quickly reprimanded him, "I did not raise you to be like this!"

Mudiwa took out his cellphone and dialed a Vaya number. The taxi service was always punctual and in less than ten minutes it had arrived just in time to witness the continued heated altercation between mother and son.

Mudiwa waved down the car and handed it to the driver.

"Take this lovely Miss home. Don't drive away until she is safely tucked inside the house and dial me up. Here is another dollar for your trouble."

KB called Thando at exactly 10 pm. The nurse attending to him handed him the phone and the long sigh at the other end of the line prepared him for the worst.

"I am holding our son's past medical records and it shows that we share the same blood type", Thando started.

"Good, did he say when he will come? Did you tell him that his daddy needs him? What did he say?"

"He insists that I shouldn't be out in the cold telling him to help some strange man who claims to be his father."

The caller on the other end dropped the line.

At exactly 11.25 am on the 20th of December 2018, KB Muzikayise died at age 60. It was exactly two days after he heard his son`s last words. KB`s autopsy report didn't mention loss of blood as the cause of death. Rather it said his heart had abruptly raptured in the most inexplicable manner. At the hospital they had cut open his chest and found a heart that had convulsed and exploded from the inside. For lack of a better word to describe it, they said his heart had broken in two... literally.

*****

Three months passed and Mudiwa's mother called him. Since the passing of KB, Mudiwa had hardly been home. The reason was simple. He knew his mother would be grieving and he did not want his beloved mother to see that he couldn't care any less about the death. The only time Mudiwa had been home was to change some clothes or get something important. This could be his driver's licence or work documents. While Thando mourned the death of this man, Mudiwa was emotionally detached from the process. Life was normal. At the age of twenty six, he was a chartered accountant by profession, thanks to his mother's two jobs; one at a mechanic shop and another at KFC. He loved his mother and he hated seeing her sad. So the last time he came into the house to change clothes - a routine normally done in her mother's absence - he left a note saying *I want to come back home.'*

So Thando called him.

Thrilled, he packed up his belongings from his friend's house and declared never to crash at anyone's house again. That had been very uncomfortable. Next,

Mudiwa headed to the flower shop to pick up a gift for her mother. He thought of getting her flowers but then again Mudiwa thought of how quickly the stuff withered. What a waste of money!

That's when he saw her. She was wearing a short sunny-yellow dress that hugged her breasts and left her shoulders bare. Her toe nails were painted white and beautifully wrapped in gold sandals. Christine was her name. As she entered the store, she swayed her long braids and gently asked for the shop assistant to help unleash her wailing child from her back. What she first noticed was the hind of his frame. He looked familiar. Too familiar.

Years of sleeping with the same person has that effect. You know them. Despite which angle they are presented, you can pick them from any spot. Mudiwa turned towards the cashier and pulled out a hundred dollar US note. He saw her and that part of his life which he had buried a year and a half sauntered back into reality within five seconds.

*****

After work, my woman always stood by the balcony waiting eagerly for me to arrive when I promised her I would be passing through. The sight of her was home. Her smile was my reason. The warmth of her embrace swallowed all my anxieties and I knew I was safe with her. Finally I get there at 6 pm and I suspect that she wants to tell me something. I think it's about our pending anniversary. Before I sit down Christine is all over me excitedly and wants to know everything. How was my week? Who did I meet? Did I miss her? What did I have for breakfast?

I want to tell her about my father but I resist the temptation. He has been dead for a year now.

I hold her steady and dig deep into her eyes and say, "Darling, we have only been apart for two days."

She hugs me and that's when I first feel it. She is wearing a loose fitting silk dress. She looks radiant and ravishing as always but then there is this presence around her. I can't put a word to describe it but it's palpable enough. I want to continue hugging her but she stops me, and wriggles her nose crazily, almost choking, "Did you change your perfume?"

"No."

"You smell different. It must be the sweat from all that travelling."

And the probing continues.

The next day, I decide to get her groceries and I text her to ask if she wants anything from the supermarket. She calls me instead and says she wants a huge bottle of Fanta. If I can get her two bottles that would be okay. Before she hangs up, she says "Darling I need a new body wash, the one I am using smells awful."

When I hang up, my mother who had travelled with me, has this gleeful smile on her face.

"Oh my god Mudiwa, she is pregnant, I say. Goodness me. Such exciting news!"

In a flash I drop my phone and remain frozen, trying to pick it up but failing.

I tell myself I am not ready for this. I know I am not ready.

*****

Christine never saw or heard from him for the next twenty-five months. Only his mother kept in touch in the desperate attempt of not wanting to lose a part of her son. Poor Thando!

The twenty-five months lapsed and they met again at a supermarket.

The baby was now a toddler who liked flowers so her mother had finally given in to her request. On that same fateful day Mudiwa had rushed inside the supermarket to pick up groceries for the weekend.

Across him at the florist's section, he overheard a conversation between a mother and daughter who were disagreeing on which flowers to buy. The little girl finally won and clapped her hands cheerfully. Christine raised her head and her eyes collided with his. The clock stopped ticking. The baby was surprisingly big now, Mudiwa observed. The resemblance with Thando was there alright. The high cheekbones and round dreamy eyes. An incarnation indeed.

"How are you?" He asked trying to appear indifferent, stealing a few glances at the toddler in pink.

"I am fine", answered Christine ever polite and calm

"How is the baby? I am asking as a friend."

"How about asking as a father?"

In his indifference, he dumped some hundred dollar notes in her hands and flew off. As he was getting into his car, a hand grabbed him and there she was. This time the polite gait was missing. Christine released the ward of cash in her hands and screamed, "We need you more than we need the money. Emotionally, psychologically, we need you!"

Dumbfounded, Mudiwa took the money and offered it to the little girl. Terrified the little girl recoiled and said, "I shouldn't take anything from strangers. It's bad."

Then both mother and daughter held each other's hands and left him. There was a sense of finality in their walk. There was an atmosphere of contentment in the way they look at him for the last time. It was at that moment that Mudiwa knew that he would never see them again. Something told him that this time around they would not look for him anymore. Neither would they wait or hope for him to return.

He felt his mother's presence engulf him. Something about this was all too familiar. It was like watching a movie he had seen before. After a hard tussle with his memory, it finally releases the familiar scene that he had suppressed. Mudiwa finally got it. It finally dawned on him why the sight of Christine leaving him alongside his daughter fetels familiar. Decades ago, his mother and he had done the same thing. After months of waiting and praying for KB to come back, they had approached him at his work place and he had simply told them, "I feel nothing for you and neither do I owe you anything. Please leave."

Those had been the words that raised him. The fatherly advice he was given and for the first time, Mudiwa realized that without actually saying it verbatim, he had repeated KB's words to his little daughter.

Immediately, within the precepts of his minds, he said out loud, "Have I become my father? Am I that man, the one person I have fought to have no affiliation whatsoever with? Am I that man?"

The moment of wisdom came and went as quickly as it could.

Christine opened her car door to let her daughter in. If this had been another time earlier, she would have broken down and cried. However, she had made a promise to herself to only cry in moments that were necessary. And this wasn't one of those moments. Unexpectedly, someone grabbed her hand almost making her drop the child. The little girl screamed,

"This strange man is after my mommy. Go away!"

Christine shook off his grip and lashed back at Mudiwa, "Are you insane, what are you doing? You are scaring my daughter."

"I don't want to be the 'strange man' anymore!" A deranged Mudiwa said in between his panting. Clearly he had run hard to catch them.

"What?"

"I don't want to be the strange man. I don't want her to refer to me as the strange man."

"Are you insane? What else do you expect? Life is not rehearsal."

"No you don't understand. The day my father called me to the hospital I referred to him as the strange man. I remember the hatred and bitterness of the moment. My daughter must not have the same fate. This is now a cycle and I don't want it."

The little girl cried even more and hid in her mother's arms. "Who is he mommy? I am scared. Tell him to go away."

Christine smiled lovingly at her child and said, "I think you just met your father, let's go home."

LINDA MASUDZE was born and bred in Bulawayo, Zimbabwe. Her first attempt at writing was with the Newsday Arts column. The positive feedback from readers catapulted her to progress further with writing stories and sharing them with the world. She is motivated by everyday lived experiences of people around her. Professionally, she is a holder of a Bachelor of Laws Honours Degree from the University of Zimbabwe.

THEMBINKOSI

Nicole Ngoma

"That's ridiculous, you can't tell me you are out of options! If it's money you need, that's not an issue", he says, opening his wallet. The man standing before me is clad in a crisp white shirt and a black tie enclosed by a tight-fitting waist coat. His pants are burgundy, and they are tight, extremely so that the bulge on his groin area is so visible it leaves nothing to the imagination. Everything about him screams wealth including the matte black Rolex watch on his wrist.

"How much?" he asks, exposing a couple of hundred United States dollar notes.

I ignore him and sigh. That's the problem with rich people, they think money can fix anything well... in his case it can't.

I almost feel sorry for him, except for the fact that I think he is already blessed enough to be complaining about an extra appendage. I mean he has a sculptured jaw, smooth dark skin, a button of a nose and a well-trimmed beard. Looking like that alone should be considered a sin, not to mention the fact that he is wealthy. I'm pretty sure everywhere he goes, he leaves women salivating.

Despite all this, I find myself drifting away to two days ago when I received that call from my brother Ndumiso. I had a sinking feeling the moment I heard how scratchy and forlorn his voice was and then he said "Thembinkosi, dad...dad has left us".

All the emotions I had been bottling up since the day I left my village, Matshetsheni, all gushed out leaving my chest tight and my body trembling. That damned man! How could he die? How could he die so early? I'm only twenty-seven for goodness sake! It's too early for me to be tied down. I'm in my prime and my career just took off. I've just become one of the most reputable doctors in Bulawayo. Ask anyone who 'Doctor G' is, they know. They know I defied the odds and became a successful surgeon at a tender age, not to mention how I have managed to strive in a male dominated field. And I, Doctor Thembinkosi Gabula, will not let that man, that dead man, drag me back there! Even as I mumbled all this, I knew deep down I had to go back there, if only for his funeral. I also knew that despite his one huge mistake, he hadn't been a terrible father. In fact he had done better than most and for that he deserved my presence at his funeral.

My father, Aaron Dingizwe Gabula, was a formidable figure in our village. He was a tall, well-built man whose favourite accessory was a smooth mahogany knobkerrie, he liked to walk with. It was a mystery why he walked with it because his back was still strong. I learnt about the significance of that knobkerrie from my eldest brother Awakhiwe, the day he made his too. I remember feeling the smoothness of its length as I ran my tiny hands over it. He was carving it under a big baobab tree.

"That", my brother said, pointing at his newly made knobkerrie, "is the mark of a man. It represents his strength and paves his way to fight the many battles of life."

I was too young to understand what he meant then, but I nodded eagerly while revealing a toothless grin. A few weeks later, I learnt another use for knobkerries as the whole village gathered in our compound to mourn the death of my mother, Sihle Ndiweni. Men came in their numbers adorning straw hats, dusty oversized formal jackets and knobkerries. My father was widowed when I was only six years old, Ndumiso was nine and Awakhiwe sixteen. The men of Matshetsheni village paid him respect alongside their knobkerries. After my mother's death, my father became sterner and very protective. He refused when my mother's family offered him my mother's young sister Nomasonto to be his new wife. This act earned him respect of my eldest brother.

I am brought back to reality by the whisperings of a crowd that has gathered around us. 'Mr. Wealthy' is fuming.

"Are you even listening to me?" he says, "You are given way more credit than you deserve, Doctor G! How can you not be able to do a simple operation?"

That last part got on my nerves, no one and I mean no one belittles my abilities as a doctor and since this man seems to be fond of creating a scene I will give him a taste of his own medicine.

"With all due respect, Sir, I'm sure you can live with three balls", I raise my voice just enough for the people around us to hear, and to my satisfaction, some start laughing.

"Like I told you before, removing your third testicle may damage your ability to have children. You just have to accept that you are a man with three balls", and with that I turn, leaving him shocked with a mouth so wide even a bus could fit.

I can feel the start of a migraine and I desperately need a glass of icy cold water. But before I can reach my office, I am intercepted by a nurse.

"Doc G, you are needed immediately in the private ward, room 43, the patient is hemorrhaging!"

I love working. I love it simply because it doesn't give me time to think, so that way my fears are kept at bay.

It's no surprise that as soon as my head hits the pillow at home, sleep takes over until a couple of hours later when I'm woken up by the sweet aroma of chicken stir fry (my favourite). I find him clad in my red apron singing along to Sam Smith's *How do you sleep'*. He is tall, muscular and has a rough raspy voice that sends chills down my spine whenever he speaks. I hug him from behind and inhale his masculine scent.

"Hey James", I whisper.

"Hi love", he responds, turning around to lift me up onto the kitchen counter.

"I've missed you", he says while crushing his lips mercilessly on mine and then using his hands to expertly explore the rest of my body. Butterflies flap in my stomach, leaving me wanting more. I grab his T-shirt while he parts my legs and moves my panty aside.

I met James in Swaziland during a cancer seminar. He had been dressed in a casual jean and a tight t-shirt that enveloped his body to perfection showing his tight abs and bulging arms. I instantly liked the fact that his casual outfit was so much in contrast with the formality of the event. It was comical really and rather very attractive. Besides, why should anyone conform to societal expectations? I certainly hadn't when I left Matshetsheni. I knew a man like that could handle anything, even me. We've been together for almost three years and I've loved every moment.

After our kitchen session, we move to the lounge where a little coffee table is set with our dinner. This is one of the reasons why I love James, he goes out of his way to make me happy. As we chat about my day, my spoon knocks on a metal something in my plate. I dig away the stir fry and there lies a shiny ring. I lock eyes with James as he reveals a wide grin and he pops the big question.

*****

I'm already halfway to Matshetsheni when the sun breaks out mercilessly, erasing any trace of dawn. I took the bus. I regret my decision for not driving when an unkempt woman drags her haggard body towards the seat next to mine. It isn't her that's really bothering me, it's the toothless infant on her hip. It's no surprise when the stench of urine wafts to my nose, indicating an unwashed nappy, as she settles next to me. I quickly open the window to relieve my poor nose. Soon, I drift to a restless slumber as memories of my childhood infiltrate my dream.

My father wasn't rich but he owned a sizable herd of about forty cows. He didn't work and so it was those cows that were responsible for clothing us and taking us to school. Life was better when we had calves, that meant we could sell milk. By the time I was nine, I had fully shouldered the duties my mother had. However, my brother Ndumiso had a soft spot for me and always helped out when he could, much to my elder brother's scorn.

"That's women's work", he would say, "let Thembi do it, you want her to embarrass us at her future in-laws?"

My father was accustomed to spending most of his time with Dlodlo, who shared my father's love for watermelons. Such that ever so often, the two would be seen face deep inside half cut watermelons, only to wipe their juicy mouths with their sleeves. Dlodlo had a daughter, Nosipho, who was a year older than me whom I had become quite good friends with over the years. I recall I would often stand on the ant hill behind the biggest hut in our compound in anticipation so I could spot Dlodlo's adeptly huge forehead. It was fortunate that Nosipho, my friend, did not inherit it.

Soon my dream took a turn, to when Nosipho and I had just filled up our water containers by the river when we heard some rustling atop the huge rock that overlooked the part of the river we were at.

"What was that?" Nosipho asks, rushing to hide behind me.

"It's probably a lizard hoping to catch some sun", I said, lifting the huge metal container to rest at the top of my head.

"Wait, did you hear that thump?" Nosipho continued, "something just fell from that rock!"

I didn't take Nosipho seriously because as long as I had been friends with her, she had always been squirmish. It was a wonder how she survived living in a village with a lot of bushes.

Just as I was about to leave, I heard a hiss, titled my head as far as the weight on my head could allow and saw the biggest blackest cobra ever. It was perched on a tuft of grass just a few meters from us. It seemed it had already noticed us too because its head was raised, exposing its wide scaly dark neck.

"Don't move", I said to Nosipho or one of us could get hurt.

I thought of a way we could escape, but I knew I couldn't do it with the water on my head.

I decided to slowly put the container down while maintaining eye contact with the snake, when I had almost reached the ground, I lost my footing and it charged towards me.

"Run", I said to Nosipho as my face met with the ground.

I could feel my life flashing before my eyes and made one last prayer, closed my eyes and awaited the inevitable. I heard a loud bang, another, and then another. I risked raising my head and saw the once alive snake laying lifeless a couple of centimetres from me.

"Are you alright?" Methembe asked, giving me a hand.

"I'm ...I'm alright... thank you".

"Were you following us again?" Nosipho appeared from nowhere.

"No, I wasn't", Methembe quickly retorted, looking away ashamed.

Methembe was Nosipho's elder brother. He was sixteen by then, I was twelve and Nosipho was thirteen. He had trouble associating with other boys his age because he was an albino.

"Were you spying on your girlfriend again?"

It was Nosipho's habitual joke that I was Methembe's girlfriend because he seemed obsessed with me. I didn't mind his attention, I rather felt sorry for him because he was always alone. It didn't help that their father, Dlodlo, was the chief. People whispered every time he passed by. I know Methembe heard some of them but he was never moved. In my eyes he was brave to withstand all that criticism. That is why on that day he saved me from the snake, I vowed to always be his friend.

Nosipho and I attended Matshetsheni secondary school. Despite Nosipho being a year older than me, we were in the same class. My primary school teachers had not seen the point of me doing grade five because I had totalized my grade four exams. By the time we were in form 2, my father did not have enough space in his hut to hang my certificates of commendation. Nosipho on the other hand, was an average student, however, her brother Methembe had passed his O'Levels immensely and was set to go to Gwanda High School.

I wasn't oblivious to the fact that I was becoming a woman; my breasts were enlarging by the second and my skirts which had once looked like sacks, finely outlined my voluptuous hips and butt. It didn't help that I inherited my mother's beauty. Methembe now looked at me differently. I had caught him too many times stealing glances at me when he thought I wasn't looking. He had also grown more protective of me. He insisted on accompanying me whenever I was going somewhere far. It was on one of those long trips that I had my first kiss.

I had been sent to deliver a letter to my aunt, NaSiko, who lived at the far end of our village. Methembe insisted we take a short cut through a stretch of bush. On our way back, my thin slippers ensnared a sharp thorn that pierced the back of my heel. I yelped in pain and sat butt down, Methembe held my foot and gently removed the piece of thorn with his nails. He kept tracing with his forefinger where the thorn had been and finally looked at me. The way he looked at me was different, it was as if he was staring right into my soul and the intensity of it made my heart beat uncontrollably. He leaned forward and placed his lips so slightly on mine, I hadn't kissed anyone before and didn't know what to do. He seemed to sense this and told me to follow his lead. He pushed my lips open with his tongue and sucked my lower lip, then let his tongue roam free in my mouth, I followed suit and soon our tongues danced to a rhythm that awoke foreign feelings in me.

The bus screeches to a stop and jostles me awake. The dirty woman has already vacated the seat next to me. As I stand, I spot my brother Ndumiso's unmistakable receding hairline opposing the traffic of passengers excited to get off.

"There you are! I almost thought you wouldn't come", he says as he reaches me, "Let's get you home."

I don't tell him how conflicted I was nor how I unpacked my bag twice with indecision. I don't tell him how I almost thought of missing the bus on purpose or of faking a severe illness. I don't tell him how scared and vulnerable I feel right now because if I do, I might cry and I can't cry. I need to be strong for what lies ahead.

"Let's go", I say determinedly.

Nothing has changed about our homestead in the last ten years. Nothing except two new huts painted in a muddy brown colour with beautiful dancing miniature figures along their bases. I don't need to be a rocket scientist to know where the money to build them came from. Several of my female relatives can be seen bustling about as their hips sway in the African print wraps tied around their waists. The men are seated on benches under two huge mahogany trees while passing around an urn of traditional beer. Shirtless children are running about the compound making the dust rise to meet the smoke coming from the fire behind the kitchen where three-legged iron pots are sprawled on the fires giving off a rich meaty aroma that make our mouth water as we enter the gate.

"Ndumiso, there you are", says a woman coming towards us.

I squint my eyes as I take her in. Wait a minute… is that aunt NaSiko? She looks a thousand years older than the last time I saw her.

"Is that 'our bride' you have there with you?" she said revealing a set of corrugated brown teeth.

"No, it's me, Thembi", I say and immediately her wrinkled face scrunches up into frown. I had expected this.

"I hope you do right by us this time around, we were disgraced enough", she says as she turns around grabbing my brother for a chore that needs his attention, leaving me all alone.

My brother turns around and gives me a look of apology. I never really liked my aunt NaSiko growing up. She was strict and stern, I wonder what her husband saw in her. In my eyes she had a heart of stone. Whenever she came to visit, she complained a lot. I couldn't sweep the yard to her satisfaction, my food was always half cooked, not to mention she always made me repeat the ironing just because I had omitted some creases. I lost count of the number of times she scolded me, all in the name of grooming me to be somebody's wife one day.

I make my way to the men first and kneel to greet them.

"Is that you, Thembi? Come here and give your uncle a kiss", my favourite uncle, Dumisani, says.

In our Ndebele culture, kisses are a sign of kinship.

"We will talk later", he says and I immediately get anxious. My next stop is the kitchen which is the hard part. If you didn't know, most women are blessed with the ability to talk excessively and unnecessarily! What an unfortunate trait that is. I know that the moment I step into that hut, my aunt would have already spread word of the prodigal daughter's return and I will be bombarded with questions.

I'm rather surprised when I am embraced as I got into the hut.

"I'm so sorry Thembi, it was his time", a cousin of mine says, and for the first time it really strikes me that my father is gone and I will never see his lop-sided smile again nor hear his hearty laugh. I will also never ask him to fix the mess he left me in. I remember that fateful year vividly. I was in form 4 and everything about my life was promising. I was set to attend the same high school as Methembe. However, fate had other plans.

Early that year, a cow died in my father's kraal. Another five died the following morning and whatever disease had killed the first finished the rest of the herd in a period of three months, the kraal was wiped clean, leaving us destitute. The rest of the year was hard for us. We were lucky to even have one meal in a day. My father thought Dlodlo was an angel but I knew better. He had bargained with me, a right he didn't have even as a father. By the end of the year my father had a new kraal with fifteen new cows. It was for this reason that I grabbed the opportunity of a scholarship to study in Bulawayo. I never told my father of it. The day our form 4 results came out, I went to school to collect them and never returned.

*****

I watch them lower him to the ground and I feel so empty and devoid of emotion. It's all too surreal. It seems like yesterday that he was standing at this very spot carrying flowers to put on my mother's grave, that is now next to his. A strong rush of emotions knocks my flood gates open. I can't control the tears as they run down my face. A hand offers me some tissue and I take it gratefully. I steal a glance at the tissue owner and Methembe is standing beside me. He is much more grown than the last time I saw him. His solemn face does not hide the fact that the past years have been kind to him. He is handsome. He notices my stare and glances at me in a way that says he understands my pain. He reaches out to touch my hand and surprisingly I don't stop him.

"Welcome back home my wife", he says.

NICOLE NGOMA hails from the outskirts of Bulawayo, Zimbabwe. She became a qualified English and French teacher in 2018. She loves playing basketball, sewing and listening to pop music. Her first novel, *Rose Mary,* and two short stories are yet to be published.

Facebook: July Rock
Instagram: nicole-ngoma

IT NEVER CAME

Aisha Sururu

I look down. The calluses on my hands have accumulated as proof that I have spent and lived my life working hard. During the harvest season, I would be part of the harvest team. After the first rains, I would be part of groups that sowed seeds. When the farms were not hiring, I took the opportunity to go into the big city and see what wonders waited for me there. I would make every effort to earn money or work in exchange for some food. I did not steal, I did not beg; I worked. I worked for each morsel of food that entered my mouth and nourished my body and that of my family. The cuts, the scars and the deep cracks on my hands testify to this.

So how did I end up here? Here, in a 2 meter- 3-meter cell with a small rectangular window above me as the only source of light. The light catches on the silver handcuffs that are around my wrists and give a little hopeful twinkle. These handcuffs serve as evidence that I have had a new identity plastered on me. I'm now labelled a criminal.

My head bowed, it sinks lower and lower with each crime the warden lists. Who committed these crimes? He then reads out my sentence, but I don't hear it; I am yet to process it. He asks me to stand. I am unable to. How can I use the same muscles I developed, whilst working hard to provide for my family, to carry my body to the gallows? It is against my instincts to walk towards my death. I have spent my thirty-eight years running away from it, yet death still managed to find me.

Two police officers enter my cell. They push me up and carry me out. Then, it starts to rain. The clouds race to block out the sun and it becomes ominously dark. A lightning bolt flashes across the horizon. How I wish it strikes me, I would accept that kind of death, not this shameful one.

I am taken back to my cell. The officers, annoyed that they would have to do this process all over again tomorrow, harshly push me in. I take the three short steps back to the wooden bench I have sat on for the past week, whilst I wait for tomorrow. Today did not happen as we all expected it would. I have gained an extra twenty-four hours to wrestle with my reality.

"Six more rains to freedom", the police officer scoffs at me. Officer Pudgy is a heavyset young man. That's not his name but it's the best way to describe him.

What Pudgy is referring to is our village's tradition. If it rains seven days in a row at the scheduled time someone on death row ought to have their sentence completed, it is taken as a sign that God is overruling the judgement of man. The criminal's charges are dropped because their sins would have been, quite literally, washed away by God's mercy.

Calling it a tradition is putting too much weight on it. Only once before has the rule been evoked; when it was made. A woman had been tried and convicted for practising witchcraft. She was sentenced to death by hanging but each day the hangman tried to complete the sentence, it rained. In those days, hangings were public gatherings. On the seventh day, those among the gathering who believed in the white man's God protested. They wanted to prevent the law from hanging her. They claimed it was a sign from the heavens because, on the seventh day, God had rested. In the case of the alleged witch, the law should rest from trying to complete its sentence on the seventh day. It must have been some protest for superstitious, traditional villagers to have banded together behind the Christians to protect someone who was charged with the crime of witchcraft! In any case, it is now a rule. A death sentence will be voided if it rains seven days in a row during the time of the planned hanging. This 'rule' was made to appease the villagers. The courts then started only carrying out death sentences during the dry seasons. This was to avoid the coincidence of rain falling during the rainy season being mistaken for God's judgement.

How did I end up here?

It was just after the cotton harvest season when I decided to head into the city to see what opportunities would come my way. As I entered the city, it felt different, its vibration frequency was no longer in phase with mine. I felt uneasy. Yet I did not leave. In hindsight, that was my first warning to head back to the village. The uneasiness was screaming out to me "you don't belong here, go back, go back, go back". If only I had taken heed. Though, I would have gone back to the village empty-handed. How can a man, a husband and a father go back home with nothing to offer? No, leaving the city with vacant pockets was never going to have been an option.

I arrived in the morning and by lunchtime my belly was grumbling. I weakly sauntered around the town going in and out of shops. Sometimes shops can have a vacancy for a general hand, or they just had a delivery and are willing to throw some coins your way to help out with the offloading. The coins may even be enough to buy breakfast, lunch or dinner depending on the time. Do meals even have their formal names attributed to them if you only have one a day?

That's how I met Madam. She was eavesdropping on the conversation I was having with the shopkeeper when I was asking if there was any labour that I could do in exchange for some money or food. I should have known then, my second warning, that all was not well. To eavesdrop on the conversation that two strangers are having, now that is not uncommon. Yet, Madam went a step further, striking up a conversation!

*****

"Stand up!" I have never noticed before how boisterous the warden's voice is. It holds so much authority. His voice is going to be one of the last voices I hear. Not the sweet voice of my wife. She's not an articulate lady. At times she says inappropriate things. Regardless, her voice is soothing, just as long as you ignore the contents of her speech.

It is a new day, a new day ready to be my last day. We go through the same cycle as yesterday and again I cannot bring myself to willingly walk to my death. After all that has occurred, I realise that I am not brave. I'm afraid of death. I spent my life trying to do all I could to avoid it. When the grim reaper seemed to be around one corner, I would head in a different direction. I went to the extent of avoiding funerals. I heard rumours that the angel of death would still be roaming around looking to identify their next target. Of course, this is false; people who have never attended a funeral still die.

*****

"May I please get a blanket or dry clothes?" I ask the Pudgy.
It rained again and more intensely than it did yesterday.
"What's the use? Whether you get sick or you don't, you're dying soon anyway."
As I shiver, I remember Madam. She is a short lady, 'petite' she liked to call herself. She wears her hair big and bold as if she is trying to make a statement or is it a cry for help that I just couldn't decipher? On the day I met her in the supermarket, her hair was milk-white. She would go on to change her hair seasonally or as she felt like it. All that hair hid her cute, heart-shaped face from the world. There is a dark beauty

mark in the middle of her left cheek that sometimes grows one or two hairs. Her nose is button-shaped and she has what would be considered a 'three head' because her forehead is quite small. It seems as if her hairline was invading her face. Her ebony skin framed an hourglass figure. Nothing was too big and outstanding, but all the parts were inadequate proportion. That first day, I could not tell how old she was because she dressed like the youth I had seen around town. Later on, I met her three children. The oldest was fourteen meaning that Madam was not a young girl anymore, despite her dressing and behaviour exclaiming otherwise.

"Hello", Madam said.

Her voice was high pitched and nasal, very unpleasant to the ear, but she smiled, which made me soften up to her. People didn't normally smile at me in the city. I quite obviously looked like an outsider, a raggedy, dirty village person. She stretched out her hand to shake mine and I couldn't believe it! Did she want to shake MY hand?

"I'm dirty," those are all the words I could come up with in my shock.

Was she not worried that my obvious poverty would be transferred to her if we touched? That she would be tainted for life, cursed to live a life of hand to mouth as I did?

She didn't mind, she shook and gently squeezed my hand; all whilst with a smile and a twinkle in her eye. She confessed that she had been eavesdropping and offered me a gardener job, right there and then. That should have been my third and final warning that something was not right. My life has never been easy. Each and everything I have done and accomplished (however little) I toiled for. Now, I entered the city and within a few hours, I met a friendly lady who was not repelled by my appearance; who was offering me a job?

"Yes, thank you", that was all I could muster in my tongue-tied, shocked state.

I didn't know where that came from? It certainly did not come from my intuition that was still screaming out to me 'you don't belong here, go back, go back, go back'. As I think back now, to those moments, it probably came from that part of me that had always just sought out death. The part that hated to work and wanted the easy, relaxed life I could not afford. That pit led me down this path, led me here.

After a long drive out of the city and into the suburbs, some twists and turns later we were at her house. She showed me around where I would be working. Arming me with a pail, a towel and soap, she marched me into the outside bathroom. There was hot water! I washed and scrubbed every nook and cranny till I felt clean. It took three buckets of water to get me clean then on my fourth and final rinse the water finally ran clear. I wrapped myself up in the big body towel she had given me and the soft, plushness of the material felt foreign on my body. She came out of the house holding a fresh pair of clothes for me. They weren't brand new, just slightly worn but those were the newest clothes I had ever worn. The blue denim jeans she gave me were too small for my 2-meter body. They ended a whole hand span above my ankles. The white t-shirt hung loosely over my malnourished body. Over the 3 months I worked for Madam, I would go on to fill out the t-shirt. When the jeans got too tight, she kindly bought me a new pair. I was completely transformed.

*****

It's weird how remembering those memories feels like I'm reliving the whole thing. I lie down on the bench. It is too short to fit my whole body. Only my torso is on it and my legs dangle from the edge with my feet planted on the hard concrete. No care at all had been taken whilst laying the cement. The jagged floor and hard, high in some places, with depressions in other spots. Some edges feel sharp so if I try to lie down on the ground, I feel the ground cutting into my flesh. So, I sleep uncomfortably on the bench.

*****

I close my eyes and let sleep take over and transport me to some relief. I remember how she showed me around to where I would be sleeping. It was a small room; I had thought so then. My new cell has redefined to me what a small room is. I had been used to the wide huts of my village. My compound there consisted of three huts. My hut, a hut for my wife and children and the hut used for cooking and entertaining guests. The room in Madam's compound was a third of the size of my hut in the village. Though, it had electricity, a basin and a tap with a mirror that hung on the wall above it. Next to the basin was a window that had no curtains for privacy. The bed stood on a metal frame. I remember the first time I sat on the bed, it was firm and comfortable, unlike anything I had sat on before.

I can still recall most of the vivid dreams I would get sleeping under the lush covers. I used to dream about the kind of future I would have. I felt like my life was finally starting. On the bench these past few days, all my dreams have been about death and my funeral that I don't think anyone will come to.

How did I get here?

*****

Day three comes and goes. Same cycle! It rains! On day four the warden comes up to my cell. Recites the list of crimes I allegedly committed. Then he reads

131

out my sentence. The only difference is that I do not have the overwhelming sense of fear today that dampened my spirits before. I think I might have come to terms with my fate that this is how it's going to end for me. Or maybe I am hopeful? I am worried about how my story will be told around the village. It will be said that I was well known for being a hardworking yet poverty-stricken man. I left for the city and got enticed by the glitz and glamour it held. That was when I felt that the kindness of my employer, Madam, was her way of trying to seduce me. So, I took what I wanted from her, violated her body and when she threatened to report me to the police, I killed her.

It rains again. This time it rains so hard that water flows into the building, and it meanders its way into my cell. I'm ashamed to say, I got onto my hands and knees and lapped at the water like a dog. I have not been given food this week. Since I was supposed to have died that first day, I have no rations. At least, that's what I was told by Pudgy. He enjoys giving me these delightful updates about my situation. He rolls over to my cell and whacks his baton across the bars of the cell and taunts me with whatever news he has.

"Four more spots of rain to freedom." This time he does not say it with as much glee as he had yesterday. His confidence is starting to dwindle with each coming day. I think I can hear the bitterness peppering his voice. Is he worried that I will not die?

Since I am on my knees already, I decide to pray to all the gods I know of and to my ancestors. It seems someone up there (or down under) does not want me dead. I take a chance and spread myself down on the cement to look up and out of the window to try and see if the sky holds any sign for me. The clouds have already cleared, and the sky is back to its beautiful blue. Will it rain tomorrow?

Grrrrrrrrrr, it is Mr Pudgy running his baton along the cell bars again. I don't know when I fell asleep. One moment feels like it's rolling into the next without any clear demarcations. Still, on the floor, I turn away from a rough edge that is piercing into me to lie on my back to look out of the window again. I usually climb onto the bench and peep to see what is going on in the outside world. I'd see other prisoners doing their time and having hope that there is an end that does not involve death. Outside is the prison courtyard where the grass grows only in patches. A disgrace.

*****

I used to work on Madam's piece of land with excellence. Her lawn was a thick lush green carpet. I would overhear her (eavesdropping? Like master like servant) getting compliments from her friends when they would come over about how beautiful her garden looked. She took all the credit for having 'trained me'. I would glow with pride that she felt so proud about my work. When I first got there, the orchard was nothing to speak of. One night I had a dream about picking oranges from a tree and eating one. As I ate it, its juices ran down my bare arm. I woke up with joy in my belly as if I had eaten one. The next morning, I presented the idea to Madam and she was delighted! That same day she showed me where 'she' imagined it should be and bought me some seeds to get me started.

*****

"Three more spots of rain to freedom." Indeed, it is raining again!

"Two more spots of rain to freedom." Police officer Pudgy spat that out. Like it was acid eating at his voice box.

*****

Each time it rained on Madam's compound; her mood would change. As if the clouds in the sky were clouding her mentally. During such days she would not dress up in her usual festive colours or wear any makeup. She would spend the whole day drinking and smoking on the veranda. I could see her from my curtainless window in my room. The day she died was raining. I only remember hearing a gunshot.

*****

"One more…" His voice trails off towards the end of the statement. He has grown less and less chipper with each twenty-four-hour extension on my life. With the way he behaves, you would think I am taking life from him.

They find me sitting on my bench. Weird how I have taken ownership of it. My head is no longer bowed. I am no longer weighed down by the charges of having killed my mistress. Yes, I was the only other person on the compound that day. The memory comes crashing down on me in this final moment. I heard the gunshot. I ran over to the veranda and found her lying in a growing pool of her blood. Her eyes locked in with mine and her lips turned into a slight smile. I tried to press down into the wound to stop the bleeding. I don't remember why, but I picked up the gun and threw it into the pool. Why did I do that? I think I feared the presence of the grim reaper still around the body. I think I feared that that part of me that always wanted to end things would rise and take control. I think I wanted to join her because she looked more peaceful than I ever had.

*****

My head is no longer bowed. I am no longer weighed down with the list of crimes I allegedly committed because I didn't! And the heavens have spoken six times before; they have come to my rescue. I hold onto faith that they will come to help me again.

Today my muscles work. I carry myself out to the gallows. I look down at my feet as I take the first step and think where will I go after this? After they let me go, which path will I follow? Another step and I think about my family and how they will be in disbelief when they hear what happened to me. One last step and I think about Madam, I wonder what last thoughts flirted with her mind before she took her last breath. I wait in anticipation for my second chance, for the heavens to clear my name.

No rain came.

AISHA SURURU was born and raised in Bulawayo, Zimbabwe. She is a medical student who loves reading and spending time with family and friends. She's an adventurous young lady who recently took on horse riding, after falling in love with horses during her horse therapy philanthropic work. She is passionate about teaching, travelling and volunteering. She is a Christian.

BLIND HOPE

Linda Sibanda

Blurred visions haunt my present yet my future looks bleak. My eyes are wide awake, blinking, yet all I can see are frozen images of cold corpses dotted on the ground, floating in a fountain of blood. I watch the events of the past reflecting vividly on the scattered pieces of glass on the floor. Nothing can pass through such solid pain and live. Is this pain or death I smell? The fresh smell of blood being sucked dry by the scorched earth haunts my memory . A cloud of darkness hovers around me replaying the bitter memories of my past. I am holding onto a thin thread that is about to break on the edge of the cliff.

Millions of questions cloud my mind, should I let go or should I keep holding on. What am I living for? Bathi *indoda ayikhali* but I am only human, I feel too. I crush and I also breakdown . How long will I hide behind this fake smile as if all is well while my last rays of hope flicker like the dying flames of the candle on my chest of drawers? I am heading straight into a thick dark mist. Will I be able to find strength let alone the courage to walk once more on these hot coals of life.
I ask myself if death is as painful as the elders portrayed it to be. I watch the pieces of glass on the floor closely. Can I do it? Narrow stripes of fear start entering me, poisoning my mind. Is this even fear or a sign from God? Can anyone be sure of such? Why then do we tremble at the very mention of the word? This fear can never be greater than the pain I have endured. I know what pain is all about . Pain is a man. A man drowning in agony and sorrows all in the name of *indoda ikhalela enhliziywweni*. Pain is when you watched your family die in cold blood paying for your mistakes. Pain is when a man watches his sisters being brutally raped and yet cannot do anything about it. The pain I

will feel after dipping my cut wrists in water is less compared to the one I felt watching my father with a tyre on his shoulders, being baptised in petrol for fending for his family. Tell me, do I have a purpose in life after this?

I will forever regret the day my path crossed with that snake which I mistook for my friend. Zwelihle Mguni. The chain of events leading to the birth of this soul sucking darkness is all because of him. His unquenchable thirst for money and blood landed me in a pit so deep it left a huge void in my life. If only I had been patient and waited for the right time I wouldn't have been here.

It was a year after the villagers had glorified my father, Mr Mlotshwa, with the title of being the sacrificial lamb. Being the man of the family after a series of suffering, in a home infested with children whose stomachs were all looking up to him, my father did what he saw best to keep us fed. He always sat my brother and I down, rebuking us from doing anything close to what he did no matter the circumstances. He kept making us promise him till the day of his death. The images of how he died are still as clear as calm waters.

The villagers coming in our compound at dusk chanting slogans carrying flame torches with the village head and able bodied man. We watched them through our broken window panes in shock while our father sat quietly on his seat at ease. He kept mumbling words which seemed like a prayer with tears streaming down his wrinkled checks. His last words: *"Boys, take care of your mother and sisters. Do not forget my teachings and keep my commands in your heart."*

He handed himself to them on a silver platter and never protested. I always blamed him for not fighting, I blamed him for handing himself in. Had he given up? Were we too much of a load for him to carry on his shoulders? Questions rattled through my mind as I watched my mother whaling behind the trail of villagers whose lashes rained heavily on my father's already cracked dry skin. Was this how a man gets repaid for keeping his offsprings alive and well? Was this how God punished his people? I watched as the villagers hanged a car tyre on his shoulders, anointing him with petrol, sending him away with harmonious curses which cemented the foundation of hatred in my mother's aching heart. Her silent cries and her pain were just but words left unspoken which never did any justice to my father's punishment.

After my father's horrific death, my mother never was the same. She became bitter and heartless with a stone cold heart darkened by pain. She turned into a corpse before our eyes tormenting our shattered lives like the ghost of Christmas past. The first thing I and other boys were taught when we were young was that as long as there is a male figure in the house regardless of his age he is the head of the house. Those were the heavy words one was meant to carry on his shoulders because of his gender. They called it responsibility while we were being victimised into suffering. Made to walk blindly into a dark tunnel of despair not knowing what was waiting for us. I can still remember the day my mother crushed my spirit, leaving my whole life sore questioning my identity.

"Mkhonzeni, how long are you going to wake up seated waiting for us to feed you? With whose sweat are you surviving on?"

"E-e- mama I--I--"

"You-- you-- what Mkhonzeni? Are you a child? You are a full grown man who can impregnate a girl any day yet you are here depending on other people like a parasite that needs a host to survive. Contribute something for a change!"

"Mama, I will wait upon the Lord for the right time and the right job. I cannot rush into things or else I might end up with bad company."

"Wait upon ini? Nyew nyew Lord. Did this same God you are praising see your father wallowing in pain, looking for food to feed your mouths? Did that same Lord save him from the wrath of the villagers?"

I gulped down the lump of pain stuck in my throat as her words took me down a memory path I had been fighting hard to keep at the back of my mind. The heaviness of my mother's words evidently blamed God for everything that we were encountering. She had obviously lost her faith.

"Mkhonzeni, this is the world not heaven. Unless your God comes down from wherever he is hiding to feed us, do what you must, as a man, for your family to survive unless you are no longer a man you call yourself to be."

"I--I--"

"Then prove yourself and stop being a tick that feeds on other people! Everyone has their own cross to carry! You are not Jesus and there is no Peter here to carry your cross. We might be a family but we are in a war and we are fighting for our lives for survival. No one will fight for yours if you don't do it. I am your mother but if a time comes where I have to keep myself going by feeding myself only, I will willingly do it. I wouldn't care less even when your starving body lays on that corner."

Stricken with pain, I fell on my knees feeling thin strips on liquid leaking on my face. I could feel the inner core of my voice trembling like the last flickers of a dying flame. I was crying. For the first time in my life I had been struck where it hurt the most. Is this what they call being a man? Having your heart crushed into a million pieces while they still tell you to follow it? How? Which piece will I follow?

Futile dreams, that is all life can offer. This is worse than blindness. There is no difference between what I see with my eyes wide open and what I see with my eyes closed. Darkness has found favour in me and chose to dwell in my household forever. Is this what fate has in store for me? Should I blame fate or myself? They say a person is made by his choices. These choices have mothered my pain, sorrows and suffering. The blood of those I cherish lay in my bare hands. I remember it all like yesterday. Zwelihle pulling up at the local shops in his car. The ants on the ground could smell the wealth he carried. I wondered and envied him like a child who had just seen sweet honey. Questions flooded but little did I know curiosity would kill the cat. My envy later led to a bittersweet life. If only questions gave birth to answers I wouldn't have followed the path I took. His words were vague but yet the truth was there before me. Is this what it is like to be blind?

"Mkhonzeni, look at yourself. How long are you willing to live like this feeding from waste like a dog? Lazarus was even better, at least he picked crumbs that fell from his Master's table."

His words were like daggers piercing through my heart. That's what I had become, a dog ?

"I can make your life change within a flash of a minute. Keep in mind what I offer is not for the faint hearted but those whose hearts are strong as Damascus Steel."

"I-- I-- I will do it no matter what the consequence is."

I wish I hadn't said those dangerous words. I wish I hadn't uttered a single word but wishes are just horses, I was driven by envy. That alone became the seed of my blindness. Zwelihle took me to a strange shrine that day. The place was adorned with red and white cloths with human carcasses dangling on the trees like Christmas decorations. The ground on which my feet stepped on inflicted torment on my already swollen feet. I could feel the thorns piercing through my skin sucking my soul out like the angel of death. The aura around it could wake a demon from the deepest pits of hell. An unpleasant looking man stood before us and his words forever torment my soul up to now.

"Ask and it shall be given to you. But for everything asked there is a price to pay. To keep the balance, once given, something has to be taken. What do you desire?"

Zwelihle nodded with a smile plastered on his face signalling me to speak. Words which paved the path of death for me. Words that led me to my pain. Did I stop? Like the fool I was, I murmured the words with pride and joy. I smiled at death as it called me.

"I want wealth and power. I want to be the greatest just like a phoenix that rises from the ashes of shattered dreams."

"And what do you have to give."

"Anything that you desire you may take."

Blind Hope is what I was given. I believed I had conquered, I believed I had succeeded but my actions led to greater sorrows. My hunger and thirst for wealth had consumed my brother. The miners coming to our house carrying just but a shirt is all we got. Nothing made sense, nothing seemed clear and let alone my heart swam in a pool of torment, fear and grief. I had taken the life of my only brother. The hard way seemed too long for me, the cross I carried on my shoulders was too heavy for me and taking a life was the shortcut I chose. The shortcut became my only brother.

Every action one takes does have consequences and mine were yet to turn my storm into a cyclone. Meluleki, my brother, haunted my dreams and my soul knew no rest. My life turned to misery while my nights became short. The dream was always the same and every detail is still printed clearly in my mind. My body laying on the bed, still unable to move. Screeching noises of a metal being pulled on the floor. Sharp painful spikes cutting through my flesh bringing forth excruciating pain to my throat. Then my body dangling in the darkest corner of the room. Hanging from the rafters with sharp thorns of barbed wire sinking deep into my already swollen neck while fresh blood oozes out from my mouth, noise, ears and eyes. Meluleki standing near the bed chanting.

"A life for a life. A life for a life", his voice echoed mercilessly in my ears bringing me to my endless nightmare. I would sit all night long waiting for dawn to strike without an ounce of sleep. That had become my new routine. My faults had reincarnated the spirit of my brother.

What is a man? What is being a man? Is there any difference between the two? A man is defined by his choices. A man is an unshaken pillar that stands tall for its family to lean on. A man is an eagle that flies across the sky eyeing for prey that has eyes on its own. An eagle that faces the storm head on until it flies above it. I question myself. Was I that man? Do I define what a man is?

I stood there frozen like a corpse while the vulture feasted on my own. I failed to rebuke him from my territory and the hyena sucked the life out of my cubs. He came just like a thief at night out to destroy. It had been a long journey of healing and continuous pain and finally my family was making peace with both my father's absence and that of my brother. Even though I had build my castle on a mountain of sand, the foundation had started to take shape until Zwelihle came once more. My sisters were singing with their sweet voices, but those melodies became the ones to pave the path to their tragic ending. Threatening to reveal my deeds before my family, he came with the price to take away my sister's innocence. They knew nothing and their pureness still shined bright like *indosakusa*. My words fell on deaf ears, my strength was challenged but tied to a tree I was. Before my eyes and that of my mother, he forced himself on them and shredded their lives with his dark soul. I saw it in their eyes. The darkness, the pain, the agony and the sorrow. Words failed me and tears wrote the whole story on my cheeks. My mother died a million deaths before my eyes. She became the definition of pain in human form. Who can stand such pain? Watching a husband burnt to death, a son's life blown from the surface of earth like ash and now watching the two prides of the family losing their souls before her eyes. Zwelihle courageously stabbed each and every one of them after feasting on them. Just like sacrifices, their lives were taken. My mother's cries did not do any justice, her pain led to her death, her grief wedged her. Just like that, a blade sliced her throat as easy as cutting margarine with a hot knife.

A wound was open and eternal pain was born. Blind Hope is what I received. Least did I know I had opened the door for the devil. All that is left is regret, pain and agony. I want to depart from life to end this endless torment.

I SHOULD HAVE WAITED. I SHOULD HAVE BEEN PATIENT. IN MY NEXT LIFE LORD, LET ME NOT REPEAT THE SAME MISTAKES. LET ME NOT FORGET THAT STORMS INDEED MAKE TREES TAKE DEEPER ROOTS.

LINDA SIBANDA is 19 years old. She was born in Kadoma and grew up in Bulawayo, Zimbabwe. She is currently studying a Law degree, with the dream of becoming one of the best judges in Africa. Linda has unshakable love for choral music, reading, writing and God.

Love and a Lie; or Two

Luzibo T. Moyo

Breathing is a natural thing. Just inhale and exhale. Let the air in, then when your body is done, let it all out. In. out. In. out. It's not rocket science, just life. I had been doing it since I was welcomed in to this world by the rural midwife. Why was I struggling to breathe though? Why were my lungs failing me? Why was my heart beating in my ears? It couldn't be because I was wearing a dress that was tighter and more lavish than I normally would wear. It couldn't be because I didn't want to be a part of the wedding in the first place. It couldn't be because I had a thick layer of makeup that made the woman in the mirror a confused stranger staring hopelessly at me. It could, however be a compilation of all the above with the additional fact that it was *their* wedding in particular. The solution was clear - Only death could save me from their wedding, and that made me question whether I was brave or stupid for putting myself through such torture.

"You look stunning, Nlenje," she said sweetly, pulling me out of my miserable thoughts and into my bitter reality. I unwillingly turned away from my reflection to face her, gave her a weak smile and replied, "Only you are allowed to be called that today, cousin. You look like an angel, honestly."

I hated admitting it, but she had always been beautiful, since childhood she had been an outstanding beauty. I was pretty sure the compliment was a norm to her. I would blame it on her family's wealth and her urban background. She always had the expensive beauty products to enhance her already breathtaking features. I made excuses for her good looks - My only way of consoling my hurt pride when all the village boys gashed over her. She was simply gorgeous. With silky chocolate skin, big coffee eyes and a statuesque figure. She looked like the people on TV and on magazines. I envied her. All the girls from our village did but they were lucky because she wasn't their cousin. Being compared to her was my lifelong curse to face.

Thankfully for me, she only visited on school holidays and sometimes she didn't at all but that never stopped the others from asking me about her. It was always about her. The private schools she went to. The gifts she got for her birthdays and Christmas. The good grades she got with the help of extra lessons my mother could never afford for me. Her scholarships, her educated father, her phone, her hair; you name it, if it was hers it got some form of worship. What kept me from hating her was the fact that she never noticed how amazing she was. She was oblivious to how inferior she made us all feel. It made me protective over her. She had my heart in her hands. The beautiful Lulamo Chimoyo; my sweet cousin.

"Well, I hope my groom finds all this..." she gestured to herself, "...appealing."

I nodded my head as I watched her makeup artist paint her eyelids with an ombre of purple hues. I couldn't speak. Especially not about him to her. I had struggled enough with the subject matter whilst preparing for this day and I prayed that the wedding would be the last time I have to. I would have to start a new life. I would have to go far and not look back. I wasn't sure I would ever forgive myself or him. The guilt was making my stomach ache as I watched Lulamo check her made up face with a proud smile. She turned to me flashing her brilliant smile and gave me two thumbs up. I nodded in approval. She always wanted my approval. It always puzzled me - why? Again, my mind would try to find explanations for it like:

She wants your approval because she has no female siblings and you're the closest thing to a sister she has – I'd think.
She wants your approval because she trusts your good character – I'd say to myself.

She wants your approval because deep down she's insecure and her confidence is a façade – I'd lie to myself.

It was probably because asking me was polite. It was out of pity. I was a poor rural woman who only knew Plumtree town and Bulawayo whilst she had been to South Africa, Botswana, Canada and England. She spoke English like a white person and I couldn't read a whole sentence without being frustrated with myself for stammering. She was tall and slender while I was short and plump. She had a prime minister for a father and my father died poor, leaving my mother and I with nothing. She had three successful brothers and I didn't have any siblings. Sometimes I wondered how my mother felt seeing her little sister living such an outlandishly luxurious life with her children. Why didn't my mother marry a rich man like Lulamo's mother did? We wouldn't be in this situation if mother had been cleverer.

"Nlenje, are you okay?" one of the bridesmaids asked and I grinned weakly.

They were all staring at me now. Had I been lost in my thoughts all over again? I looked up and found that; Lulamo had managed to wear her gown and the makeup artist had finished packing her kit. The other bridesmaids gave me awkward glances and one of them was actually glaring at me. I was an outcast. These were elite women who were used to the extravagant purple dresses they wore. I was uncomfortable in mine. It followed my body leaving a large portion of my breasts on display and it hugged my bottom as well as my hips. Plus the high heels were killing me. I was sure they could smell my poverty and lack of class.

"I'm fine I just need water", I answered nervously marching out the bridal dressing room, their eyes burning my back as I walked out.

Finally I stepped out and felt a change in the air. I could breathe again. I was alone in the hallway, palms sweating and hands shaking but at least I could breathe again. I took a few more steps away from the door then leaned against the wall. I could hear them giggling, laughing and chuckling with Lulamo when the door closed. I knew they weren't talking about me but it felt like they were. I felt like a laughing stock. I knew I was being ridiculously paranoid because none of them knew. But still...I knew and that all it took. I knew it all and I felt as though I wasn't hiding it well enough. I decided to walk down the hallway aimlessly. I had to calm down before I exposed myself. They couldn't know what power they had over me. They couldn't find out how much they hurt me. How had my life come to this? A series of wild emotions ranging from the calmest to the most passionate. I wanted it to end. Once they married it would all be done with.

I heard footsteps from behind and turned to find the white wedding planner on her way to the dressing room. She smiled and told me not to take too long as the ceremony was about to start. Without waiting for my response she disappeared into the dressing room. I exhaled, rubbing my stomach and fighting the tears that burnt my eyes. Then I chuckled, I had never been to a Zimbabwean wedding with a wedding planner, let alone a white one – more evidence of my cousin's posh lifestyle.

A moment later the makeup artist walked out of the room and waved goodbye as she passed me. I just waved back. I didn't want to go back into that dressing room. They would have to find me in the hallway waiting for them. Then I heard another set of footsteps before a male figure stepped out of the men's restroom.

It wasn't just any male though. I knew his silhouette. I felt his aura. It was him.

Philani Andrew Khumalo. The love of my life. The apple of my eyes. The man of my dreams. My strength and my weakness. My illness and my remedy. My damnation and my salvation. I hated the sight of him, but I couldn't take my eyes off him. I knew that this was how Eve probably felt about Adam. I just gazed at him, taking him all in. His stubble, his high cheekbones, his hooded eyes and his thick lips. I took all of him in, every last bit as if I hadn't memorized his features already, many times before. Maybe it was because I knew it would be the last time I would look at him without fear of being caught. Or maybe it was because the emotions he provoked in me, froze me. He looked up; as if sensing my stare and his enchanting eyes met mine. The impact almost dropped me to the ground, knees weak, air knocked out of me and the void growing deeper in my heart. I was his victim, and I wasn't sure I'd ever stop being one.

"Nlenje…" he pleaded.
I shook my head, swiftly turned to leave but he ran to me and grabbed me before I went far. Damned stilettos.

"Leave me alone, Philani", I barked out.

"We need to talk, Nle."

"About how much of a lying cheating good-for-nothing you are?" I questioned.

"It's not what you think, Nlenje. Let me explain."

"I don't have time to listen to you lie to me, Philani. You're about to marry my cousin. There's nothing to talk about", I snorted.

"Could you let me talk, please? Just listen. I know you've been avoiding me since you heard of my engagement to Lulamo. But you have to understand this marriage is a business alliance. Her father is the prime minister of Zimbabwe, not to mention the CEO of Chimoyo Enterprises. My family owns the biggest transport company in Zimbabwe. It's a powerful move marrying us. Beneficial to both families and businesses. But you have my heart, Nle. You know that..."

"No, Philani. Do you think I was born yesterday? I've been avoiding you because I knew you'd come up with these excuses. These lies. You've been seeing her for some time now and was probably never planning on marrying me like you promised. I was just your parents' maid who you could use as a play thing whenever you felt like it. I was just a source of gratification, wasn't I? And now you're going to marry the other woman in your life...the one you've been saving for marriage. You're a sick man, Philani. A cruel, twisted man. Let go of me", I shouted, but he didn't let go. He just pulled me closer.

"Calm down, Nlenje. They're going to hear us", he whispered.

"Like I said before, I don't have time to listen to your lies. If it's true that this is an arranged married, why didn't Lulamo tell me? Why would you choose money over me in the first place, if you love me like you say you do?"

Silence.

"Exactly what I meant by excuses, Philani! You're so cruel. You used me. You convinced me for months to be yours, selling me dreams and lies for the last two years. Keeping me a secret from your family because you were ashamed to be involved with the house-help. And now that someone more educated, beautiful and wealthy has come along, you're throwing me away like a used condom? How would you feel if I left you for a richer man? You chose money over me, our love, our future and our child. So sorry if I'm not in the mood to be manipulated or lied to. We could've been a fami..."

"Wait...what do you mean our child? Nlenje, are you pregnant?" he asked, bewildered.

"Was... I *was* pregnant", I corrected smugly.

"What do you mean *was*?"

"I...had a miscarriage", I lied.

I had an abortion – I thought – *but I want to hit you where I know it will hurt.*

"The stress of losing you made me lose our future. Our child, Philani," I continued, glaring at his dumbfounded expression. Then it sank in and I could see the pain in his eyes. I knew how important family was to him. I knew he looked forward to being a father. I knew at that moment he regretted not fighting for our love. He always told me he wanted to marry me then we would have children in our own house and spoil them rotten. He told me I would give him beautiful children. It broke my spirit when I discovered I was pregnant because it was a few days after I heard of his engagement to Lulamo. I had already started avoiding him. I couldn't let myself be that woman in his eyes. That woman who used being pregnant as a way to keep a man. My morals, standards and pride couldn't let me. He had made his choice and if I couldn't be his first priority then I wouldn't make him stay out of pity.

"Nle, if I had known..." he choked and I felt as though my heart was being torn from my body.

The dressing room door opened and the wedding planner froze when she saw us. We were standing so close, both our expressions showing the negativity we had lost ourselves in. she cleared her throat awkwardly before ordering Philani to head to where they would exchange vows. Then she turned to me and told me to help Lulamo in the dressing room.

From then I couldn't see anything. I was numb. I was lifeless. Just drifting through the whole process. One minute I was walking into the dressing room after my conversation with Philani; the next I was watching them take their vows. I didn't know how to feel about everything Philani had told me about this wedding being a scam. It didn't make me feel better and knowing it was arranged didn't change the fact that it was happening. I was powerless. Smiling like a Barbie doll.

Just keep smiling – I thought – *just look happy, it's only for today.*

When my eyes met my mother's as she sat next to her sister; the mother of the bride, I could tell she felt bad for me. It angered me. What was it about me that attracted pity? I felt my anger boil beneath my skin.

"Does anyone here object to this matrimony or have reason as to why they should not be legally and spiritually bound together?" The Bishop asked.

Silence. I exhaled.

"Beautiful. In that case let us proce…"

"Stop!" a man shouted from the entrance before marching down the aisle.

Everyone looked astonished. The journalists started taking pictures. Women started whispering. Mr. Chimoyo's bodyguards walked up to him and grabbed him violently. My heart was pounding. I couldn't breathe all over again. People were gasping and the bride looked scared.

"Lulu, my love, I know you're pregnant with my child. I love you, baby. I don't care if your father doesn't approve of our love because I'm white but I love you. And I love that child in your womb. Our child. I will fight for you and for our child. Don't get married to him please. You're supposed to be my wife, Lulamo and you know it", he kept shouting as the security struggled to drag him away.

He was like an enraged bull. They couldn't tame his flame. He was brave and brazen. I turned to look at the bride and groom. They looked both distort. The bride's father was so angry one could almost see stream coming out of his ears. My eyes searched the whole room. So many different facial expressions on people's faces. From intrigue, suspense, curiosity, to shame, shock and anger. It was a full range of emotions.

"I love you, Lulu. I know you love me too. I may not be good enough for your father but I know I'm good enough for you my love, please. Don't let me fight for us alone. I need you. I need our child. Don't go through with this..."

I watched the strange white man with red eyes and yellowish hair declare. I envied Lulamo more than I had ever done before. I watched her run towards her lover and collide with him, leaving Philani at the altar; stone-faced.

Everyone watched as the prime minister's daughter ran off with her white boyfriend leaving her wealthy groom staring at the distance. The irony of it all...my sacrifices. All for nothing. I had given it all up, for nothing.

Once again; I was a fool.

LUZIBO TABONA MOYO is the author of **Love and a lie or two**, her first published work. Luzibo was born and raised in Bulawayo, Zimbabwe. She was a singer-songwriter before shifting to short story writing and has published on Wattpad under her stage name-alter ego, *"Luchi Shiki"*. She is also a fine artist and is currently practicing as a resident artist at the National Art Gallery of Zimbabwe in Bulawayo.

luchishiki@gmail.com
@luchi_shiki

The End